MW00480011

The Great Journey

A Kingdom Divided

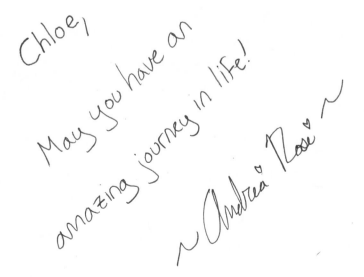

Chloe,
May you have an
amazing journey in life!

~ Andrea Rose ~

Books by Andrea Rose

The Great Journey Series

A Kingdom Divided   (Spring 2011)
A Legacy Continued   (Winter 2011/12)

The Great Journey
A Kingdom Divided

By
Andrea Rose

HMSI
Publishing L.L.C.

Plymouth, MI, U.S.A.
www.PublishHMSI.com

The Great Journey – A Kingdom Divided

The Great Journey Series
Book One

Published by HMSI Publishing L.L.C., a division of HMSI, inc.
www.PublishHMSI.com

By
Andrea Rose

Copy Editing by
Natalie McAllister

Cover Design by
Chelsea Popa

Publishing Coordination by
Jessica A. Paredes

Published by
David R. Haslam

ISBN – 13: 978-0-9826945-4-1
LOC: Pending

0083-0001b

Printed in the United States of America

TKR 10 9 8 7 6 5 4 3 2 1
MK 31527-23898
40752 21:25

To my parents and brothers

Chapter I

Castle Hemlock and its superb architecture stood towering over the surrounding kingdom. Every inch of this castle was a masterpiece, from the gleam of the golden doors to the ornate stone carvings that covered its walls. Every step further into this castle led to more treasure for the senses to behold.

Outside in the courtyard, the crisp smell of autumn filled the air. Despite the season, the landscape was as lush as ever. The trees were showing off their array of colors as succulent fruit hung from their stems, ready to be picked and placed upon the king's table in feast. There was no sight more exquisite to behold than this. No sight, that is, except for the king's one and only daughter.

She was even more beautiful than the summer roses from the castle courtyard, whose beauty was such that all the peasant women would be wooed into marriage by any man lucky enough to sneak a single perfect blossom past the palace guards and into the hands of his love. The king's daughter spent most of her time in the courtyard, and her face glistened from the sun. She had dark, slightly lavender eyes and hair of dark silk that flowed down to her knees. Not a man in the kingdom could resist her charm, but she was not one to fall in love easily, for the Hemlock family had many enemies.

Today was a decent day for the Hemlock Kingdom, but for the Hemlock Kingdom, a decent day was not a good day at all. The rebels were advancing to one of the major centers of commerce in the kingdom, the city of Vhaldai. Vhaldai was known for its great defenses, since it was one of Hemlock's major arms producers. Vhaldai was strong, but the rebel forces were high in numbers and thirsty for blood. The rebels were more than willing to die for their cause; to take the current ruler of the Hemlock Kingdom off the throne and put their leader, a once loyal follower of the current king, on the throne. Vhaldai was fully aware that a fight was sure to come, a long and arduous fight that could only be ended by bloodshed.

The daughter of the king, Princess Victoria Jane Hemlock, was outside in the castle courtyard. In the center of the courtyard was a small pond filled with exotic fish. A fountain of a cherub holding a jar with water trickling out stood in the center of the pond. The pond was surrounded by an assortment of shrubs and flowers, and just beyond lay a stone bench with circular patterns carved into it. The princess lay on this bench, her face pointed towards the sun. She was wearing a long, flowing gown made of the finest silk. It was the color of a soft pink rose, intricately outlined in gold, and it flaunted the princess' slim figure. She lay there, humming to herself. Birds flew by, stopping on the branches of nearby trees to sing along with the princess.

The church bells began to sound. This mellow chiming told the princess that something was wrong, so she abruptly stood up and began making her way towards the church, her gown flowing behind her.

As she passed by the east castle stairwell, she heard a sickly coughing. At the top of the stairs she could see her father, the king, with two servants helping him around. Her father was ill, but there were high hopes that he would get better. This was important for the Hemlock rule of throne, since the Queen had died many years earlier from sickness and five of the king's nine sons had already died in this terrible war with the rebels. Princess Victoria shook the thoughts of the bloody war from her mind and continued on towards the church.

At the entrance of the church, Victoria found herself walking past her uncle, Vincent Randall Hemlock, who was just leaving. He had lived at the castle for as long as Victoria could remember. Vincent was dressed as fancy as ever, with fine silk robes, a freshly trimmed beard and his dark brown hair combed back. He was tall, with a long face that always seemed to show a blank expression. Her father would reassure her that this was his way of dealing with the pain and loss dealt by the war. Vincent not only had to deal with the loss of his nephews, but had also encountered death in the battlefield on the few occasions he had chosen to fight.

As the princess entered the church, she noticed many visitors were on their knees in tears, and in the very front of the church lay a body on the casket bench, limp and lifeless. The Priest stood by this body, praying for the soul's safe delivery into heaven. When Princess Victoria noticed the royal emblem on the tunic of the body, she feared the worst. Her shy walk turned into a fast trot, then a full on sprint.

Lying there in front of her on the casket bench was the youngest of all her brothers, Prince Benson Daniel Hemlock. His once lively face was now pale and still from death. The princess held his hand as a single tear fell from her cheek. His hands were cold, and she noticed a small patch of blood soaking through his silk top near the center of his chest. She knew he had suffered a painful death.

The same sickly coughing as before was then heard at the entrance of the church. The visitors' prayers grew silent while they watched the king of Hemlock make his way to his youngest son's dead body. Princess Victoria did not turn around, but instead continued staring at her brother. She let go of his lifeless hand.

When her father finally reached Prince Benson's body, Princess Victoria watched as he touched his son's cheek with the back of his hand. His face was cold, so the king took his hand away in shock, only to reach back towards his son to move a lock of golden hair from his face.

The king turned away from his son. "It was a necessary death," coughed the king as he walked away.

Princess Victoria, angered by her father's remark, turned around and watched him stumble down the church isle.

"That's it?!?" she yelled.

The king froze, but did not look back at his only daughter.

"Benson is dead and all you can say is, 'It's a necessary death?' How many more Princes must this Kingdom lose? How many more brothers must I see lying dead? How many more sons will you send to their death in this dreadful war?!?"

The king stood still, as if he had something to say. Instead, he raised his hand and waved to his servants to help him to the door. He understood that his daughter had not only lost a brother, but a best friend as well. Victoria stood by Benson's side. She watched as her father disappeared through the church doors. She was left alone to deal with the death of yet another brother.

Chapter II

Victoria had not spoken to her father in five days. Just being in the same room with him made her feel sour. She had heard rumors about the death of another Prince, but she could not bring herself to believe that she had lost yet another brother. She reasoned that if another prince had died, then the king's soldiers would have already brought the body back. She lay in the courtyard day after day, listening for the mellow church bells. All she could hear was the singing of the few birds still left this early in winter. Still, Princess Victoria felt that something terrible was soon to come.

A few weeks after Benson's death, she heard the mournful sound of the church bells. By this time the first snows were beginning to fall on the Kingdom of Hemlock. The princess sadly made her way to the church, expecting to see the lifeless body of yet another one of her brothers. Instead, the church was empty, except for a few birds flying high about the ceiling.

Princess Victoria walked to the front church benches and took a seat. The cushions were made of a soft, red satin, which felt good against the princess' skin when she rubbed her hands nervously over them.. The rest of the bench was made of a strong, dark wood. The princess then folded her hands together.

Victoria began whispering to herself, "Please protect my family in these times of war. Lord, keep my living brothers safe and give peace to those who have already passed on."

She was abruptly interrupted when the church doors swung open.

"Princess?" shouted an out-of-breath voice.

Princess Victoria raised her head and looked around to see who was calling her name. It was one of the Palace Guards, with a dark brown, scruffy beard and gleaming gold uniform. His sword hung from his belt on his right side. She had seen him in the Castle before, but could not recall his name.

"Princess, come quick!" he shouted as soon as he spotted her.

The princess stood up and ran to follow the guard out of the church, for she knew that when a Palace Guard came to the church grounds, something awful had to have happened. After all, soldiers were known to prefer taverns and training halls to church pews.

Princess Victoria found herself outside of her father's room, being coaxed by the servants to go inside. Despite not having talked to him in quite some time, she entered his chambers.

The King was lying in bed, his sickness plainly worse than ever. He was in the midst of a coughing fit, and it was easy for anyone to tell that he was in pain. His pale face was tinged with green and the bottoms of his eyes sagged. His usually clean shaven face was now covered with patches of stubble. He was dressed in his nightgown, and his strained expression revealed the extent of the pain in his body.

Princess Victoria walked towards her father as his servants slowly helped him sit up in his bed. She held his hand, noting that it, too, was a sickly color.

"I'm afraid the doctor was wrong," said the King in a slow, hoarse voice.

"Father..." whispered the princess, but her father cut her off.

"He says I have but a month to live."

At this point, Princess Victoria was in tears. A slow, steady stream rolled down her cheeks and onto the side of her father's bed.

"I have sent word to Alejandro about my sickness," continued the King. "As my oldest son, he is to come back to the castle immediately and take over the throne. He will watch over you when I am gone."

"Father," started the princess once more. "I'm sorry I yelled at you. I'm sorry I ignored you! I'm so, so sorry!"

She leaned in and started to cry on her father's weak shoulder. He slowly wrapped an arm around her to give her a hug.

"No," said her father. "He was not only your little brother, but your best friend as well, and I let him go to battle knowing that he was not ready. I am the one who is sorry."

With that the King waved to his servants who came to the princess' side to escort her out. She reluctantly left the chambers, looking back only once, knowing all too well that this may be the last time that she would see her father.

Two days later, her second oldest brother, Robert Chris Hemlock, was killed. Many came to pray for the body as they had done for Benson. When she went to see the body, Princess Victoria cried even harder than ever, realizing that her father did not have the strength to bid his second oldest son farewell.

Chapter III

A month came and went in the lands of Hemlock, and their ever-faithful King passed away one cold, mournful night. The Castle kept the secret of the king's death, for it was important that the rebels did not know that Hemlock was now weak and without a king. Alejandro, who should have been told of his advancement to the throne weeks ago, never did show. The princess was stuck making many of the important decisions for the kingdom in her brother's absence.

Many nights the princess would wander in the streets by the Castle, hoping to find some peace and quiet from all the chaos within the Castle walls. She knew her ladies-in-waiting would watch her wandering, should anything happen that required alerting the guards, but occasionally she could slip away into the darkness, escaping their meddling eyes.

It was on such a night as this that the princess' life took an extraordinary turn. As she wandered the streets, away from prying eyes, she heard two men whispering. The low tones of their voices were bothersome to Princess Victoria, so she waited behind an archway in the street to eavesdrop on their conversation.

"Roma, is it time?" asked one man in a high pitched voice that reminded Princess Victoria of her brother's voice when he was nearing manhood.

"No, sunset tomorrow," replied the one called Roma.

"Sunset we attack!" said the younger man in an excited, slightly louder voice.

Roma shushed him "Not here, Manual. We must not let anyone know. Only then will we be able to successfully kill the king and his only -" a noise in the distance caused Roma to silence himself.

Two street guards came down the street from the direction of the castle. She crept further into the darkness of the arch. The guards walked by, not noticing anything amiss. They held their staffs high proudly.

As the guards passed the two mysterious men, they exchanged a brief hello, then went off on their way.

Once Princess Victoria was certain she was alone on the street, she left the protection of the darkness and, in fear for her life, ran all the way back to the Castle, never looking back.

Chapter IV

Inside the princess' bedchambers, Penny, the chambermaid, was readying Princess Victoria's bed. Victoria ran in, choking on the words she had to say.

"Penny? Penny! I need your help immediately!"

Penny stared at the princess, unsure of how to respond to this surprising plea. Princess Victoria opened her dresser and pulled out a gown reserved for special occasions. It was made of the finest silk, dyed a royal blue that faded to the color of the sky where the dress ruffled out. Diamonds studded the neckline, adding even more elegance to the gown.

Princess Victoria held the gown up to Penny, as if seeing how it would look on the maid. Penny, confused, stopped what she was doing to figure out what Victoria was up to.

"For me, my lady?" Penny asked tentatively.

The princess did not respond, so Penny stood there, staring at the gown Victoria held next to her.

Penny, though just a chambermaid, was a beautiful girl. Her hair was soft as cotton and nearly as long as the princess'. She, too, had black hair, but her skin was much paler. She did not have the luxury of time to spend in the sun as the Princess did. Victoria nodded as she made her decision. Penny would have to do.

"Penny, there's to be an attack on the Castle tomorrow at sunset. They plan to kill anyone in the royal family that they can find. I am in danger and must leave to find Alejandro and you must stay here as me so the people of Hemlock do not lose hope," Princess Victoria informed her chambermaid.

Penny, now understanding what the princess was up to, asked, "But my lady, why leave tonight when you can leave tomorrow and have the sun accompany you on your journey?"

"The rebels are just outside the Castle walls, disguised as loyal citizens. I must move now, at night, for I shall have the protection of the darkness to help me escape."

With that said, the chambermaid slipped into the gown the princess had handed her. The princess slipped into one of her older, rattier gowns. It was made of soft cotton and was the color of a dull green moss. She wore this gown on days when she trained with her champion horse, Albay.

Princess Victoria explained what Penny was to do as she used her special powders to make Penny's skin more like her own. When Victoria felt satisfied that the servants and guards would believe Penny to be the princess, the two bid goodbye to one another and the princess made her way to the empty church.

Princess Victoria went to the benches in the front of the church and gave a final prayer to protect her on her journey outside the Castle walls. She prayed for her people, and she prayed that her two remaining brothers would be safe and that Alejandro would finally take his place as the king of Hemlock.

She stood up and made her way to the giant cross that stood at the front of the church. It was made of silver, polished so finely that she could see her long silk hair flowing behind her as she walked up to it.

Just past the cross was an ornamental shield bearing the family crest with two swords crossed on the front. The princess, as quietly as possible, removed one of the swords and gripped her hair in her right hand. With her left hand, she swiped the sword across her hair and let it fall loosely to the ground. She picked up the hair off the ground and stuck it in the small fire that burned just below the shield.

After returning the sword to its place, she stood back in front of the cross to inspect the damages that had just occurred. Her once knee-length hair that had taken her a lifetime to grow was now just above her shoulders, a site that the princess remembered only from her younger childhood years.

Victoria, no longer recognizable as the princess, made her way to the commoners' stables to find herself a horse for her escape. She traded the diamond and rose quartz bracelet she had forgotten to remove for the best stallion in the stable, a golden chestnut horse with a single white star on his forehead. Fortunately, the stable boy was too excited at the sight of the bracelet to question its origin. Victoria's new stallion was named Golden Sand, after the sand found in the Sandero Plains just west of Castle Hemlock.

After saddling Golden Sand up, Victoria jumped on his back, eager to leave the Castle grounds before midnight. With a nudge of her feet and a simple tug of the reins, Victoria and her new stallion were off. Though Golden Sand had traveled many times before, this would be Victoria's first time ever leaving the protection of Castle Hemlock.

Chapter V

It wasn't until the sun was high in the sky that Victoria decided to stop and take a break. She dismounted Golden Sand by a babbling brook; the water so clear one could see the small stones at the bottom. The water made a delightful melody as it splashed past these stones, even though the brook was partially frozen over.

Golden Sand munched on the little bits of grass still visible by the edge of the brook while Victoria used her hands like a cup to sip water until she had quenched her thirst. She then wrapped herself in her cloak and lay back in the snow to rest while Golden Sand continued eating.

Victoria's stomach growled and she realized that she hadn't eaten since dinner the night before. She looked around for any edible plants that may have managed to survive the cold of winter. Unfortunately, there were none. She would have to use some of the meager provisions she had managed to throw together in her haste before fleeing the castle. She opened the cloth bag and took out a chunk of cheese and tore off a handful of bread. Not the tastiest meal, but it was better than nothing.

Victoria stood up and brushed the snow off her cotton gown. She breathed some hot air onto her chilled hands to warm them up. She patted Golden Sand just above his right hind leg, and the two crossed the brook and continued on their way.

Victoria and the stallion passed a flat area filled with many small, bare shrubs. Soon, they entered a wooded area. The trees were thick enough to block out the snow, but the sun managed to peek through. Next, the two crossed another brook, but snow covered every inch of the banks. Finally, just as the sun was starting to set, Victoria could see a little village in the distance.

Victoria hopped on the back of her stallion and raced to the village in hopes of finding much needed food and shelter.

When Victoria arrived at the village inn, the raggedy old innkeeper was kind enough to take Golden Sand to the stables for water to drink, oats to eat and hay to lie upon. Victoria, exhausted from her unexpected journey, wearily entered the inn.

The innkeeper ran a weathered hand through his thick, gray hair as he considered his newest customer... He was curious why a lady would be traveling alone, but decided it best not to run off any potential customers. After viewing the marvelous stallion Victoria traveled with, he concluded that she was a customer worth keeping and set about to make certain she would stay.

The common room of the inn was poorly lit and currently vacant. Victoria squinted her eyes to make sense of this room, but could only get a good sense of the fireplace and an adjacent table. It was easy to tell from the unkempt environment that the old couple rarely had customers. She felt her wrists, making certain her movements remained concealed by her cloak. It was then that she realized she had no jewelry, coins or other precious valuables to pay for a stay at the inn. Even so, she was unable to resist when the innkeeper's wife, an old and dainty lady, offered to cook up some food. Soon Victoria was satisfying her hunger with a dinner of ham and eggs.

After Victoria ate her much needed meal, the innkeeper's wife offered to draw a bath for Victoria. Victoria accepted, hoping to wash away the grime from her first day of traveling.

While Victoria sat soaking in the battered yet sturdy metal tub, the innkeeper's wife sat in a wooden rocking chair by the lit fireplace nearby. She was a sweet-looking lady, with dull blue eyes, thin lips and a slightly larger-than-normal nose. Her bright silver hair was tightly wrapped in a bun just behind her head and she wore a dingy cream dress.

"What is your name, deary?" questioned the old lady.

"Victoria," responded Victoria, hoping the old lady wasn't going to question her much further.

"What a beautiful name," said the old lady. "I have a granddaughter by that name." The old lady continued rocking. Victoria said nothing.

"Where are you from, Victoria dear?" began the old lady once again.

"I'm done with my bath now, thank you very much," responded Victoria politely, making it clear that she was done talking. She sat up in the tub and the old lady stood up, grabbed a slightly tattered bathrobe, and wrapped Victoria in it as she stood out of the tub.

"I hung your dress over the fire and it's still warming up," said the old lady.

"I'm fine for now, thank you," replied Victoria.

The old lady escorted Victoria to a small room. Inside was a mat laid out on the floor with a single sheet and a flat pillow. This was supposed to be where Victoria would sleep. To the right of the mat was a small, rickety wooden side table. On the table were a few lit candles, the only source of light for the room. The flickering of the flames gave the room an eerie glow.

The old lady nudged Victoria inside. Victoria didn't want to appear rude, so she knelt down on the makeshift bed and gave a half smile to the innkeeper's wife. She smiled back and left, closing the door behind her. Victoria was left alone in the tiny, shabby room. Victoria was scared. She had no idea if she had been followed, let alone how she was going to pay the innkeeper. She sat while thinking of ways to sneak out of the inn without paying. Then she began thinking of where she would go once she left. So many unanswered thoughts came to her head, and she found herself praying in hopes for a sign.

After a few minutes, the innkeeper knocked on the door to give Victoria her now warmed gown. Once the old man left,

Victoria locked the door to her room and changed into the clean gown. Exhausted, she lay on the mat and covered herself with the sheet. Within minutes, she had fallen into a deep sleep.

Chapter VI

Victoria awoke the next morning to the delightful smell of breakfast. She made her way downstairs to where the old woman was cooking up some ham with honey drizzled on top over the inn's main fireplace. In the morning light, Victoria was able to take in more of the scenery of the common room. Across from the fireplace were a long, wooden counter and a half dozen stools. Behind the counter stood the innkeeper, surrounded by an assortment of barreled ale, ready to be dispensed and served.

Though the innkeeper noticed Victoria the moment she entered the common room, her interest was in the young male who sat on the furthest stool at the counter. His hair was light brown and his face had been freshly shaven. He had tattered clothes that were a pale blue color, most likely discolored by the sun's harsh rays. By his feet lay a well-worn tan bag. Victoria figured he must be some sort of traveler who was just passing by this small village and decided to stop for some food and a drink. And yet, without being able to identify what it was about him, Victoria felt that there was more to this man than first met the eye. Since she did not yet know his name, she thought of him only as The Traveler.

Victoria decided to sit next to this mysterious male. He had chosen to eat at this infrequently visited inn on the one morning that Victoria also happened to be there. Perhaps he was the sign she had so desperately needed. The Traveler did not seem to notice Victoria's presence.

The old lady, realizing Victoria had come down from her room, turned away from the fire. "My dear Victoria," she started. "Your breakfast is nearly ready."

Victoria gave the old lady a forced smile, for now she had finally realized that she could not escape her inability to pay for the services she'd been receiving at the inn.

The old lady placed the ham upon two plates and gave one to each of her customers. Victoria picked at her food for a bit, and then stated, "I have no way to pay for your kindness except by giving you the stallion that you have taken such good care of in the stable."

The Traveler, who had tore into his meal with enthusiasm, nearly choked on his food upon hearing this. "That's *your* stallion in the stable?!?" he blurted after swallowing his latest bite.

Victoria nodded a yes, and then took a few bites of food, content that her possible sign had finally noticed her.

"What a marvelous stallion," he continued. "Too bad you ran him near to exhaustion. I hear he lay in the hay pretty much all morning. They're marvelous creatures that need to be respected."

Victoria, offended by this statement, became defensive. "How dare you judge me like that! I was only trying to escape danger, and the stallion was rather lucky I chose him for my journey!"

"Unlucky, you mean," he retorted under his breath.

Victoria was infuriated at this stranger. She stood up, grabbed her plate of food, and moved to the other end of the counter. Perhaps she was wrong about this man being her sign. The Traveler watched as Victoria moved away.

"Well," The Traveler started the conversation once more. "If you don't want your stallion, I'd be more than happy to buy him from you." At this moment, the young man reached into his pants pocket and pulled out what appeared to be a nearly flawless ruby. Victoria estimated it to be about the size of her pinky finger. He placed it on the counter.

The ruby was very tempting, but Victoria knew she might need her stallion in her travels. She informed him that her horse was not for sale.

The Traveler gave a frown, then moved his attention to the innkeeper. He slid the ruby across the counter towards the innkeeper and told him, "This should more than pay for me and this lady. Now, be a gentleman and go get her stallion saddled up for when she has to leave."

The innkeeper stared wide-eyed at the ruby. He greedily picked it up and ran off to the stables. The old lady followed him, asking to see the beautiful fortune that now rest in their hands.

Victoria looked up at this mysterious man, unsure of how to react to what had just happened. He just smiled at her.

"The name's Michael," he said. "Michael James Rundy."

"Victoria...uh...," Victoria paused for a second, and then continued. "Victoria Anne Benson."

"OK, Victoria," replied Michael.

For a few seconds, an awkward silence fell between the two. Victoria began wondering if maybe he really was her sign. She was scared, penniless and sick of traveling alone.

"Since it appears you are without a horse and I happen to have one, would you mind if I accompanied you on your travels?" Victoria asked. She was relieved when Michael accepted her companionship.

She had never traveled beyond the castle walls. Without a guide, she could potentially end up in an endless circle or worse, back at the castle where the rebels were looking to have her dead. Victoria felt much less stressed just knowing she would no longer have to travel alone. The innkeeper entered to let the two know that the horse had been saddled up and was ready to go.

Chapter VII

After a week of travel, Victoria finally had the courage to ask Michael how he had obtained the ruby. Michael was reluctant to talk about it, attempting to change the subject and sidetrack Victoria's thoughts. Victoria was just as obstinate. Finally, Michael gave in.

"I stole it, okay? There, now you know. Happy?!?" grumbled Michael.

Victoria was stunned, pausing in her tracks. She had been traveling this whole time with a thief! She began to wonder if he could possibly be a rebel, if this man who treated her with so much kindness as Victoria Anne Benson could be trying to kill the Hemlock in her blood.

"Oh, don't act like you've never stolen a thing, Miss 'best stallion in the stable'," Michael responded to her silence.

"I have never stolen a thing in my life," Victoria scoffed, grabbing Golden Sand's reins from Michael and walking ahead of him.

"Don't mock me!" scoffed Michael, sourly. "You have a stallion worthy enough to have come from the Castle Hemlock itself, yet you're wearing rags and can't even pay for a single night's stay at a shabby village inn. You *cannot* tell me that you have never stolen a thing in your life!"

Victoria did not respond. She did not know what words to say that wouldn't tip Michael off to her true identity. She was hurt, so she looked at the ground and began kicking the snow covered stones that lay in her path.

Michael could tell that he had upset Victoria and attempted to make things better by apologizing.

"I'm sorry," said Michael. "I...I shouldn't have stolen that ruby. It was the wrong thing to do, but I...that bastard had it coming!"

Victoria stopped walking once again and Michael paused alongside her. She stared into his eyes, a hard stare that nearly caused Michael to look away.

"That 'bastard' might have had a family!" Victoria argued.

Michael grew mad at this response. He had dealt with many awful people before, but at that moment, he was nearly convinced that Victoria was the worst.

"He had a wife, three hunting dogs, fifteen servants and two houses. He was the Nobleman of the small village I grew up in. He forced the whole village into labor so his wealth would increase. My mother was ill. We had no money to pay for a doctor's care, so I had to take the rubies!"

Victoria could not believe it at first. All her life, she believed the Hemlock kingdom to be a fair place. All the Noblemen she knew would never do such a thing. Her Uncle had been involved with affairs such as this, overlooking small villages to protect the citizens from such situations. Her expression, somber at first, suddenly looked puzzled.

"Rubies?" she questioned. "I thought that one from the inn was the only one."

"I left the rest of the rubies with my mother and a doctor just outside the small village where we met. The Nobleman's guards were looking for me, not my mother. It was best we split up," replied Michael.

"Oh, I'm so sorry," said Victoria, feeling sympathy for him and his mother but displeased that he stole from his lord. She began walking again, kicking the stones on the ground once more. She didn't know whether to show anger or sympathy towards Michael, so she chose the latter.

"Maybe next time you won't be so quick to judge people, now will you?" Michael stated, staring at the road ahead.

Victoria didn't respond.

"Look, I'm sorry, too," Michael explained. "I shouldn't have accused you of stealing your stallion in the first place."

Silence.

"For what it counts," Michael continued, "I've had a great time with you so far."

After a few moments, Victoria responded, "yeah, me too..."

And the two continued walking down the path in quiet thought together.

Chapter VIII

The sun had finally set and Michael was feeding twigs to a small fire he had managed to start up while Victoria searched for anything edible in the surrounding land. In the palace courtyard, this was usually an easy task. Unfortunately, the thick blanket of snow that now lay on the ground had killed off most of what was left of the autumn harvest.

Victoria's tattered gown caught on a branch and pulled her down to her knees. She mumbled under her breath as she stood up, wiped the snow from her gown, and pulled herself free of the branch. Michael, having seen the whole event take place, could not help but laugh.

"You think this is so easy?" Victoria asked. "You think you're so great, well why don't you find us some food?!?"

Michael snickered as Victoria kicked the snow in distress.

"Come on and sit down," Michael told Victoria as he patted a now warmed spot of ground by the fire.

Victoria sat down and gave an upset sigh. Michael reached into his worn bag and pulled out a small cotton sack. He opened it up, revealing an array of dried fruits and nuts inside. He took a nut, placed it in his mouth, and held the sack out to Victoria. Victoria gave a half smile of gratitude and took a small handful of the fruits and nuts. The two sat there in peace for quite some time, munching away at what little food they had while the fire crackled and jumped in front of them.

Finally, Victoria spoke.

"What all do you keep in your bag?" she questioned, hoping to start a conversation and break the silence. She was curious to learn more about this traveler.

"That's none of your business," Michael snapped back.

Victoria looked back into the fire. She was not about to get into yet another fight with her traveling companion.

"I'm sorry," started Michael. "It's just...I lied about my mother..."

Victoria was stunned. Was everything he had told her earlier a lie? She didn't respond. Instead, she listened.

"Everything I told you before, about the Nobleman and my mother falling ill, was all true," Michael continued. "But I lied about leaving her with a doctor."

Now Michael pulled a simple urn from his bag.

"The doctor couldn't save her," he continued once again. "All the rubies in the world couldn't have saved her from the backbreaking work Sir Tobran forced upon our village. When I was a young boy, Mum always talked about how much she wished she could have her ashes spread across the Vhaldishian River...it's all I can do for her now.."

Michael picked up the urn and packed it back into his bag, followed by the now nearly emptied cotton sack.

"I'm sorry," said Victoria. "I also lost my mother to a terrible illness when I was a little girl" she told Michael. Victoria couldn't help but feel responsible for his mother's death in some slight way. After all, it was the duty of the King and the Hemlock family to protect their citizens and bring a stop to corrupt Noblemen such as the one who had taken the life of Michael's mother. Victoria wanted to reassure Michael that she would never let it happen to another citizen again, but she knew she couldn't let him know that she was of royal blood. Instead, she continued watching the fire.

"So, you've been taking me to war-torn Vhaldai and you weren't even going to tell me?" Victoria questioned Michael, slightly upset that he had kept where they were heading a secret for so long.

That's when thoughts of her oldest brother, Alejandro, flashed through her mind. What if word of his father's death never reached him? What if Vhaldai had been captured by the rebels and what if Alejandro was a rebel captive, or worse, dead? So many 'what-ifs' filled her mind that she knew now that fate had led her to Michael James Rundy, whether she liked it or not. She knew she had to go to Vhaldai to find her brother and tell him of their father's fate, of the attack on Castle Hemlock, of her daring escape and unplanned journey to Vhaldai.

"How much longer until we reach Vhaldai?" Victoria asked Michael.

"Five days, maybe a week," he responded, eyes scanning the horizon in watch.

"Then we leave first thing in the morning," Victoria stated as she lay on the ground next to the warm fire. She closed her eyes and drifted to sleep, where she dreamed she was back in the palace courtyard playing in the summer's breeze with her youngest brother, Benson.

Chapter IX

Victoria awoke early the next morning to the smell of cooking meat. She looked over at the fire, where Michael was turning what looked like a rabbit over the fire.

"I caught it this morning," Michael boasted proudly when he noticed Victoria's puzzled expression.

"Rabbit?" questioned Victoria.

"Delicious, huh?" replied Michael.

On a typical day, Victoria would not have agreed. Rabbit was more of a commoner's food. She was used to fancy feasts of fresh poultry and exotic fish. Right now she was hungry, and Michael had caught them a rabbit. Rabbit was beginning to sound and smell good.

When the rabbit had been fully cooked, Michael ripped off a fair chunk of meat, and handed it to Victoria. She gave a half smile, unsure if she would enjoy this meal, and took it from Michael's hand. She tasted a small piece of the meat. It exceeded her expectations, and she began eating quickly and greedily. Unable to slow herself down, Victoria found herself nibbling the last bits of meat from the bone, something that was usually reserved for the dogs in Castle Hemlock.

"I cannot believe you were a peasant," Michael told Victoria.

"What?" she asked between mouthfuls.

"Well, it doesn't really matter, but I was wondering why you chose to become a traveler?"

Victoria stopped eating, wondering how to respond.

"I don't believe I chose this path," Victoria finally replied. "I think fate chose it for me." She took the final bite of her rabbit and threw her bones into the dwindling fire.

Michael didn't respond, but finished his rabbit and chucked his stick and a few bones into the fire as well. The two packed up what little belongings they had. Michael kicked dirt on the fire until it went out while Victoria readied Golden Sand for their departure.

A dark cloud was rolling in from the East so the small group of travelers: princess, thief and stallion, continued west, more determined than ever to beat the snow and reach Vhaldai in one piece.

Chapter X

After a few hours of traveling, the storm finally caught up with them.

It was a terrible blizzard. Hail the size of small pebbles rained down on the travelers, stinging their faces and hands. The wind blew in gusts at them, making it nearly impossible for the trio to continue their journey.

Michael, having experienced his fair share of bad weather, knew they were not safe in those elements. He pulled Victoria and Golden Sand to a thick area of trees. It wouldn't fully protect them from the wind or hail, but it would have to do.

Victoria had never been in such terrible weather. At the Castle, she would watch the winter storms come and go as she sat by the fireplace in her room while sipping cups of warm spiced ale. She always wondered how those stuck in the storm stayed warm. She never imagined that she would one day find out firsthand.

Michael found a decent sized tree and kicked a small hole in the snow at its base, putting the large trunk between them and the wind gusts. He led the shivering Victoria to this hole, and she sat down in it and brought her knees to her chest to keep warm. Michael brought Golden Sand to the side of the tree and covered him with a tattered tan blanket that he pulled from his bag. Then he sat next to Victoria, who snuggled close to Michael for warmth. He covered them both with his cloak. They would have to wait out the storm and try to survive.

Chapter XI

In early afternoon, the storm finally subsided. Victoria was trembling from the cold. Michael had been caught in worse storms before, but it was clear that Victoria had not. Without him, she would have perished in this storm. More than ever, he began to wonder how Victoria came to be traveling alone and seemingly without purpose. She was a mystery in more ways than one.

Victoria tried to stand, but fell over in the snow. Michael picked her up and sat her on Golden Sand's back. He wrapped the tattered blanket that had protected Golden Sand around her.

Michael took the horse's reins and led him and Victoria back to the path they had been traveling on before the storm rolled in.

After a while, the travelers found themselves in a clearing that stretched for miles. With the dark storm cloud still in the distance, the sky was a menacing gray. A fog hung in the clearing, making it rather difficult to see.

The clearing was easy enough to traverse despite the impaired vision of the travelers. Victoria, still trembling from the cold, pulled the blanket tight, even covering her face. She trusted Michael to lead them in the right direction.

Slowly, she felt Golden Sand come to a stop. She loosened the blanket around her face to see what was the matter. Michael was focusing on something not too far off in the distance, so Victoria adjusted her gaze to look as well. They had come upon a tent camp. Michael and Victoria were uncertain about the camp, so they approached with caution.

At the outskirts of the tent camp was a dark maroon-colored flag high on a wooden pole. The center of the flag was a white skull with a crack coming down from the top of the head to just between the eye sockets. A golden crown with the decoration of a black serpent with large, white fangs adorned the skull. Victoria stared at this flag in fear as the skull gave a menacing look back. She could feel her heart pounding in her chest as panic surged inside her. This was the rebels' flag.

"We need to turn back," Victoria said, just loud enough for Michael to hear.

"Don't be crazy," he replied upon seeing the flag. "These people can help us!"

"No they can't!" Victoria said, slightly louder this time, fear in her voice. "We can't talk to them. We just...need to leave."

"How would you know? You haven't even met these people!" Michael challenged, with more than a hint of exasperation.

"Give me the reins to my horse," Victoria demanded through gritted teeth.

The two remained there for a few minutes, arguing whether it was best to leave or stay.

"Fine," Michael shouted. "Leave! I don't understand, but go if you must. You won't survive out there alone, you know. "

"Do you want those people to kill me?!?" Victoria accused, not thinking about whether this might reveal more than she wanted to about her identity.

"Those 'people' won't hurt you!" Michael said incredulously, not seeming to notice Victoria's slip.

"Tell that to my dead brothers!"

Then silence, their words echoing throughout the camp.

Michael shook his head in frustration. "What are you talking about, Victoria?" The two stared, angrily, at one another.

Muffled yells came from the camp. The two turned their heads in the direction of the noise, only to view a horde of men with an assortment of weapons running in their direction. Victoria froze in fear. She was certain these men were coming to kill them. Michael, on the other hand, took a few steps towards the men and began waving his arms in greeting.

"Don't kill us! We're fighters for the cause!" he shouted.

"Who is your king?" questioned one of the men, upon reaching Michael.

"King Vincent Randall Hemlock, brother to the current king, but true ruler of all," Michael responded.

In that instant, it all became clear to Victoria. The rebels were led by her own uncle, the same man who had spent years in the Castle as Victoria and her brothers grew up. This explained all the corruption within the Hemlock kingdom that Michael had been talking about. Her uncle abused the trust of her father by allowing this corruption to take place. It must be a ploy to convince his followers that the current king was untrustworthy and needed to be stopped immediately, no matter the cost or bloodshed. It was no wonder the rebels seemed to know her father's every move; they had a man on the inside. Her father had once told her that he believed the rebel leader to be a once-loyal follower, but had he suspected this level of betrayal?

Suddenly, Victoria felt an arm grab hers and pull her off her horse. She fell on the cold snow only to have the same brutal arm pull her to her feet.

"Who's your friend?" the male questioned Michael, all the while making certain to keep a tight grip on Victoria's arms. Victoria squirmed relentlessly in hopes of freeing herself.

"Victoria. Trust me, she's harmless," Michael answered, a hint of humor in his voice.

"She don't look like no rebel," came the male's reply.

At this moment, Victoria was pushed to her knees. A worried look fell across Michael's face as the man brandished a club and raised it above Victoria's head. Victoria could see Michael rush forward and raise his arms in an attempt to stop the club in its descent, but it was too late. Victoria blacked out.

Chapter XII

When Victoria awoke, she found herself in a small tent with a tiny fire crackling upon a stone fire pit near the tent entrance. She was lying on a high bed, made from a mound of soft dirt.

There were other beds in this tent; mats laid out on dirt mounds. She counted three other mats, two of which had occupants laid upon them, fast asleep.

Victoria sat up and felt a throbbing pain in the back of her head. The details from the evening before were fuzzy, but she remembered enough to piece together a timeline. She thought she was going to be sick.

She quietly stood up and made her way to the entrance of the tent, slightly dizzy. She checked the two other sleeping occupants and determined they must have been peasant women. Victoria was worried knowing she was in a rebel camp, but she felt relieved that the men from last night did not recognize her true identity. She stepped outside.

Victoria could tell it was early morning by where the sun was in the sky. She must have been asleep for quite some time.

She looked around at the rebel camp. There were at least fifty tents in that one camp alone! Men with chain mail and swords, axes, daggers, bow and arrows and an array of other weaponry walked past as Victoria viewed her surroundings. There was no one to prevent her from leaving her tent, so she decided to take the opportunity to take a walk around the camp.

Finally, Victoria caught sight of what appeared to be some makeshift stables. She made her way to them in hopes of finding either Golden Sand or Michael. Sure enough, Golden

Sand was inside munching on some oats laid out before him. Another horse was being saddled up by a portly male in tarnished chain mail.

The man gave Victoria a stern look, as if he wanted her to leave the stables immediately. Victoria did not leave, but instead walked over to Golden Sand and patted him on his star. He continued munching away at his oats, but whinnied happily in recognition. Victoria ran her hand down then up the stallion's back as she inspected him for any injuries. There were none, so she gave Golden Sand a happy pat on the head. He neighed approvingly in response.

By the time Victoria was finished inspecting her stallion, two powerfully built men had entered the stables on horseback. They dismounted and started to relieve their horses of the extra weight of their saddles. When they noticed Victoria, they seemed upset at her presence in the stable.

"What might a lady be doing in these here stables?" the scruffier of the two asked Victoria in a thick accent. Victoria figured he must have come from one of the many villages of the high Moorg Mountains in the outermost lands of the kingdom. He was also very tall, and Victoria did not like how he used his height to appear as if he towered over her.

"This is my stallion," Victoria replied, attempting to make herself as tall as possible.

"Oh, of course he's your stallion!" responded the second man, sarcastically. He nudged his friend and the two of them gave a low chortle... Victoria shrunk back as she noticed the features of the scruffy male. He had a scar that crossed over his nose, unpleasant eyes and yellowed teeth. She wished he would stop laughing so his yellow teeth would once again become hidden.

He patted Golden Sand just above the left hind leg as the other male continued chortling at Victoria's earlier response. Golden Sand kicked and neighed in disapproval at this. Victoria stood tall once more.

"He doesn't like you," Victoria told the men.

The tall man, now annoyed, warned Victoria. "Calm your beast, lady, before he upsets the lot of them horses!"

"Then leave him alone!" she barked back.

Once again Victoria found herself being laughed at. Her head began throbbing. She had to think of some way to get these men to leave her alone.

"This stallion is my responsibility," she informed the men. "His owner is Michael Rundy, and he won't be happy once he finds out you've been harassing his horse. Actually, maybe he will be happy to hear it was you two, especially since he loves putting feeble men such as yourselves in their place!"

The two men, unsure whether Victoria was telling the truth, gave a scowl. They decided it would be best not to find out if this burly Michael, supposedly more robust than either of them, existed.

Victoria, nervously hoping her story sounded believable, calmed Golden Sand. To her relief, the two men turned away to attend to their own horses.

"Women these days," grumbled the scruffy man's friend, just loud enough for Victoria to hear. They left the tent, leaving Victoria alone with the man she had originally noticed.

"Don't mind them," he said in a thick accent while he finished saddling up the horse. "Most women here...they don't often allow them in the stables."

"I saw the look you gave me when I first walked in here," Victoria told the man.

"No, no, no," he whispered to himself, taking off the saddle he had just put on his horse and readjusting it. "Didn't know you were taking care of that there horse. Stallion, you say. Don't like it when we get them random wanderers about, is all. The name's Daniel. You?"

"Victoria," she answered.

"Then I will see you at dinner, Victoria," replied Daniel.

With that, Daniel hopped on his horse and took off, giving Victoria no chance to respond. She walked out of the stables behind Daniel, watching him ride away. She had not planned on staying at the rebel camp much longer, let alone until dinnertime, but she was beginning to change her mind. Perhaps it would be helpful gaining more knowledge of this camp before continuing on towards Vhaldai. After all, she was still weak from the blow to her head. She eventually convinced herself that one more night in the rebel camp would be fine.

She continued wandering through the tent camp. Dinner wouldn't come for many hours. Until then, it was important that she find some food to hold her off until dinner while keeping an eye open for Michael.

Finally, she spotted a tent crowded with many people, both men and women, who were being served a decently warm breakfast. She made her way over to this tent, content that she, for once, blended in with the hustle and bustle of a busy crowd.

Chapter XIII

It wasn't until the sun had fully disappeared over the horizon that the feast began. An enormous tent was set up at the center of the camp, a task that had taken thirty men nearly all day to accomplish.

Victoria could hear the sweet melody of music coming from inside the tent as the smells of succulent ham, savory soups and bitter brews filled the air. She began swaying to the music as she walked towards the tent, more eager than ever to meet up with her new friend at the dinner, hoping to find out more about the rebels and their plans.

Suddenly, Victoria felt a large, heavy hand at the center of her chest, pushing her and breaking her stride. She looked up, only to discover that this hand belonged to an even larger man. He lowered his hand and rested it on the sword that dangled from his left side.

"No unattended ladies," he informed her.

Victoria felt a sick feeling bubble up in the pit of her stomach. Had she waited all day just to find out that she could not come to the feast?

A hand landed on Victoria's right shoulder, giving her a surprise.

"This fine lady be with me," said a familiar, uncomforting voice.

Victoria looked over to the owner of this voice, only to find it was the scruffy man from the stables. She shrugged his hand off her shoulder.

"Are you with O'Rourke?" the large man questioned Victoria, gesturing to the new arrival.

"No!" Victoria was about to respond, but she caught herself. She needed to think! She stepped away from the unpleasant man the guard referred to as O'Rourke. He, for his part, chuckled in amusement. He knew she couldn't enter without him or some other soldier to accompany her. If she wanted to eat badly enough, she just might have to be his 'lady.'

Victoria looked over at the large tent and yearned desperately to be allowed inside. She wanted to learn more about the rebels and this camp.

"No way would I miss this wonderful dinner!" Victoria corrected herself, forcing a smile. O'Rourke howled loudly and offered his arm, which she reluctantly took.

"So you are with this man?" the large man questioned Victoria a second time.

Victoria was silent, and then gave a forced, "yes."

"Too bad for you," mumbled the guard, letting them pass through the entrance flap of the tent. The comment only served to increase O'Rourke's humor.

"That's me lady!" he said as he wrapped an arm around Victoria.

The moment the two entered the tent, Victoria pulled away from O'Rourke. He looked surprised and was on the verge of asking her what was wrong when she abruptly walked away from him before he could do her any harm. Victoria quickly lost herself in the crowd of rebel warriors and their 'attended' ladies.

Chapter XIV

Victoria had been wandering by herself at the dinner for about an hour, searching for Daniel or Michael. She occasionally listened in on the brisk chatting of the other 'attended' ladies, but the topic of their conversations did not interest her in the least. She was too distracted by the one thing she had on her mind: finding Daniel to learn more about this rebel camp.

Finally, Victoria conceded to herself that she needed to rest. She had abused her injured body quite a bit today, with as much walking and snooping she had done since waking up. On top of that, it was simply exhausting to try to hide in the open, in constant fear that someone would discover who she really was. She sat at one of five long plank tables that held most of the guests once the food was served. One end of the row had the feast, even though some of the ladies took it upon themselves to retrieve the food for as many of the rebel soldiers as they possibly could.

On the other side of the tent was a rough stage. It was large, but only a foot or so high. This made it hard for the people at the far ends of the tables to see the musicians. However, they could certainly hear them. Pretty decent craftwork, Victoria thought, for less than one day's work.

"Is that the lady Victoria?" a familiar voice with a thick accent asked from behind Victoria.

She rose from her seat and spun around to greet Daniel with a smile. She gave a friendly curtsy, and motioned for him to sit down next to her.

"Nice of you to make it to this dinner," he told Victoria, smiling back. "This one is very important! I noticed they were keeping unattended ladies out. How did you manage to get in, I wonder?"

"Thank you for inviting me," Victoria told Daniel, using her courtly manners, almost forgetting that they might give her away. "I had the help of the noble O'Rourke," she said, her voice dripping with sarcasm. Daniel hooted and slapped his thigh in appreciation of that.

"And you managed to get away? That's a rare one indeed!" Daniel's laugh was kind and Victoria realized that she felt safe in his presence, although she knew little about him and had no good reason to trust him. She had to remind herself not to forget that this man, pleasant as he was, was plotting to put her uncle on her father's, now her brother's, throne.

The two sat down. Victoria saw this as the perfect opportunity for a conversation.

"This camp is astonishing! It must be fairly new," Victoria started.

"New? Been here four months. 'Twas only short term, or so we thought. That's why it's still in progress. We thought we'd be all the way to Castle Hemlock by now, but that's the way of war I suppose. " Daniel continued. "This camp is nothing!"

"You mean, there are more camps than this one in the kingdom?!?" Victoria questioned, shocked by this revelation.

"There are many more, my lady Victoria. You think a throne can be won with only 5,000 men? It takes many more than that, m'lady" Daniel said somberly.

"How many more camps are there, then?"

"That depends on how the battles end," Daniel started. It appeared to Victoria as if he were counting in his head. "Two more in the high Moorg region," he began, as if counting the camps to himself. "Three, including the one just past the mountains. Four more are scattered in the large forest regions just South-East of that terrible King's castle...maybe there be a few others..." He fell silent once again, concentrating on a point somewhere over Victoria's head. Then he finally faced Victoria to give his finally tally. "I will tell the lady there are about ten or eleven of these camps. Some are larger; some are smaller, if that is helpful." Daniel, happy to feel as important as he did at that moment, sat tall and straight in his seat.

The 'terrible king' comment, almost caused Victoria to blow her cover to defend her father. She hadn't realized how hard it would be to keep her identity secret. It went against her very nature to let a slight against her family go unchallenged. Before she could dwell more upon it, a trumpeting of horns filled the dinner tent. Victoria looked up to see what it was all about.

The tent grew quiet as Daniel gave a simple nudge to Victoria and whispered, "This is it!" His face was bright with anticipation.

"This is what?" Victoria questioned back, starting to feel slightly alarmed that she had no idea what was soon to take place at the feast.

"This is the moment, where we get to meet our king!" came Daniel's excited reply. He and the rest of the rebels within the tent stood up, facing the tent entrance in great anticipation.

It took Victoria a few seconds to understand what he had meant.

"Vincent Randall Hemlock!" she whispered to herself, as it hit her like a bolt of lightning. She was suddenly furious with herself. She should have recognized the signs that "royalty" would be present at this feast. After all, she knew the protocol followed in her country when guests of high honor were to attend.

Daniel gave a smile at Victoria, but instead of being comforted, Victoria thought it menacing. She felt trapped. Thankfully, Daniel turned his attention on the tent entrance once again. Victoria stood up, ready to make a quick escape. She could fool a whole rebel camp into thinking she was one of them, but surely her uncle would recognize her for who she truly was if he was given such an opportunity. Victoria was angry with her uncle for betraying his only brother, but a camp full of rebels was no place for her to confront Vincent on this matter. She had to leave, and she had no time to waste.

The music had stopped at this point, and Victoria realized that everyone had turned toward the tent entrance. She was the only human in the tent still facing the stage. A drunk man seated a few seats down from her left noisily reminded her to turn around. She turned quickly, so as not to be singled out again. Once the room was calm, the trumpeters played yet another tune as the tent flaps opposite the stage flew open, revealing a bearded male figure adorned with fancy clothes and jewelry. This was Vincent, wearing none other than the clothing and jewelry that he had stolen from his brother's collections.

Vincent began walking the aisle way, which happened to be the one in which Victoria and Daniel were standing. He appeared to be inspecting the faces of his followers, and Victoria could feel her heart pounding away inside her chest as he drew closer to where she sat.

On impulse, Victoria deftly slid underneath the table while everyone else watched Vincent. Not for the first time, she was grateful that she had a slim athletic build. She firmly ignored a sudden thought about how soon Daniel would realize she was gone and the possibilities of what he might do as a result.

The floor under the table was awful. Spilt brew had made the floor sticky and half-eaten food covered what bit of the floor the brew had left untouched. Victoria, having never smelt anything as repulsive as dirty floors mixed with women's dirty clothes and men's sweaty feet, lost a bit of her food on the boot of an unknown rebel. Luckily, the man was still too fixated on Vincent to pay any attention to this.

Victoria continued crawling towards the main tent entrance as Vincent made his way to the stage. Victoria managed to spot a rip in the tent that was clear of any guards who may have tried to stop her. With everyone still gazing upon Vincent as he made his way to the stage, Victoria made a quick but quiet dash to this rip, which was fortunately just large enough for her to slip through. Vincent turned to face his followers, unaware that his greatest enemy had just slipped from his grip, into the dark of night.

Chapter XV

Victoria pulled Golden Sand from the stables and led him to a vacated area on the outskirts of the camp. Here, she quickly prepped him for their escape. Victoria worked as rapidly and quietly as possible.

Everything had become all too clear to Victoria. All Vincent had to do was make certain of the king's death, and secure the deaths of the king's children and the throne would be his. Once this was achieved, he would have the power to do as he pleased. He already had the loyalty of the rebels, and as a member of the royal family, he had the blind loyalty of the gentry of Hemlock. It was a devious plan, and Victoria could not let him get away with it.

Just as Victoria prepared to saddle up, a hand softly landed on her left shoulder, spooking her. She screamed, turning around to swipe the hand away from her shoulder, ready to fight for her life.

"Hey, it's only me," said a familiar, friendly voice.

Victoria raised her head and took a glimpse at the person's face, realizing it was Michael.

"Thank God it's you!" Victoria was so relieved that she hadn't been caught by the guards that she threw herself into a stunned Michael's arms. The feeling passed, and she released him awkwardly and reached for Golden Sands' reins.

"Where are you going in such a hurry?" he asked her. "Why were you so scared?"

Victoria didn't respond, but fiddled with the harness a bit. Michael tried a different tack.

"It would be most unfortunate if you missed out on meeting our future king," he said, with a kind smile.

"You just don't get it, do you?" Victoria sadly shook her head. "I'm not a rebel like you. I could *never* be a rebel like you."

Michael stared at her, with a puzzled look on his face.

"I don't understand you," he started. "You're supposedly some poor farmer's daughter or something, and you must have lost your family to be traveling alone. Why would you scorn our cause when all we fight for is an end to the corruption of the so-called-nobles?"

Victoria, after hearing her friend say this, realized he would not understand unless she told him the truth about everything, including about her true identity. Having made her decision, she did the one thing she had been trying so hard and so long to prevent.

"My name is not Victoria Anne Benson, Michael. I am Princess Victoria Jane Hemlock. Vincent Randall Hemlock is my uncle, and he is corrupt in more ways than you or I may ever know. My father, the King of Hemlock, placed Vincent in charge of affairs that included dealing with corrupt Noblemen, such as the one who worked your mother to her grave. I do not know how, but he successfully blinded the rest of us from their corruptness while reassuring us that all was peaceful in the land. If you wish to pass the blame to anyone within the royal family for your mother's death, then blame Vincent."

Michael blurted out laughter, as if Victoria had just made the whole story up. He looked at Victoria, expecting to see her laughing as well. Instead, her serious expression remained unchanged. Michael's laughter was cut short.

"My God," he said, staring into Victoria's sad eyes. "You're...you're telling the truth?"

Victoria hopped on Golden Sand, grabbing his reins and turning towards Michael.

"I'm sorry, Michael," she started. "I wish I had known about my uncle before it was too late for you mother. I wish I had known before it was too late for my brothers, who died protecting the kingdom they loved." Tears started to fill her eyes. "I wish I had known, but I cannot change that now..."

"Victoria," Michael faintly spoke.

"The information I gave you, I told you as a friend. What you do with it – who you tell – is up to you. I just ask, if you truly are my friend, that you give me at least an hour or so in advance before you tell anyone."

Victoria used the left sleeve of her dress to wipe away the tears that had spilled down her face.

"I promise," said Michael, lowering his head towards the snow-covered ground.

Victoria gave a half smile, a nod, and a tug of the reins, and with that she was back on the trail that would hopefully lead her to her oldest brother. If only Victoria could inform Alejandro of Vincent's treason, Vhaldai might have a fighting chance in the battle that was soon to come – That is, if her uncle didn't find her first.

Chapter XVI

Michael never had a huge role in the rebellion. He was simply another follower who approved of the rebels' cause and everything he once thought they stood for. He sat on one of the makeshift beds in the tent that had been assigned to him. His head hung low, his hands cupped over his face as he tried to understand the events that had happened earlier that night.

It was hard for him to believe that he had been traveling with the Princess of Hemlock the entire journey, yet when he recalled all the silly little things that Victoria always did, things that he could never imagine a farmer's daughter ever doing, he wondered how he hadn't figured it out earlier. Vincent would be done addressing the camp any minute now. Michael had to make a decision about what to do with this newfound information about Victoria, and he needed to make it soon.

Trumpets sounded from the direction of the dinner tent. Vincent must be leaving the feast. Michael thought back to his journey with Victoria, to all the fun they had had together and all the troubles they had shared. He also felt a feeling of anger swell up inside him when he realized that this 'friend' had lied about everything; her name, birthplace, family...but had she lied about enjoying the friendship the two had found with one another? No, he felt certain that their friendship was the only real thing between them, despite the lies they told each other. He supposed that in her place, he would have done the same thing. And in a way, he had, hadn't he?

Not everything was clear to Michael, but in that instant, he knew what to do with this information. He stood up from the bed, gathered all his belongings, and made his way to the tent entrance. He paused for a second, and after reassuring himself that he had all his belongings, slipped out the front of the tent.

Chapter XVII

It had been a few days since Victoria started on the trail, and she had not seen or heard any signs of other humans. If Michael had gone to her uncle with her secret, surely he would have caught up to her by now. Nonetheless, Victoria still could not feel at ease while alone in an unfamiliar wilderness.

Victoria and Golden Sand stopped for a rest by a small tributary. Signs of spring were starting to show in the land, and the water in the tributary seemed to dance about in celebration. Little fish swam back and forth in the water, and Victoria even managed to catch a few for her meal, meager as it was.

Victoria was getting used to being in the wilderness. Before her journey, it had never been required of her to know how to make a fire. After having watched Michael do it many times during their travels together, she was becoming a professional at it. She made a fire by the tributary's edge and placed the small fish she had collected on a rock beside the fire to cook.

Golden Sand grazed on the grass that peeked out from underneath the winter's dwindling snow. Victoria poked at the fire and began humming a familiar tune to herself, one her father would sing to her before their days of trouble began. On occasion, a bird or two returning from the south would rest on the branch of a nearby tree and join in on the song. Victoria, for the first time in a long time, was at peace. She found herself able to shut out any thoughts of the rebels and simply recollect the harmony of the kingdom before the war.

Just as Victoria closed her eyes and started daydreaming of being back within the palace walls, a distant yell came from further down the trail.

Victoria jumped up, looking in the direction of the sound, but she saw nothing. She knew she had to find a place to hide. She did not want to meet anyone who might recognize her. She grabbed the flaming stick she had used to poke at the fire, and led Golden Sand to a thicket of blackberry bushes growing some distance from the trail. She had to make the horse lie down, which was not usually an easy task. However, the horse seemed to sense her desperation and complied rather easily.

Victoria heard the men coming up the trail and finally caught sight of three men on horseback. They were making no attempts to be silent, considering that they conversed with one another by yelling across the short distance that separated them. Victoria squinted her eyes to get a better look. All three men wore tarnished chain mail. One of the men, the one furthest from Victoria, had a maroon flag mounted in the harness. Victoria recognized it as the rebel flag.

Her heart fell. Had Michael informed her uncle of her journey after all? Were these the men that her uncle had sent off to find and kill her? If this were so, then why were they coming from the opposite direction of the rebel camp?

Victoria lay still, unsure of how to address this situation. The men on horseback were making their way closer and closer to Victoria and Golden Sand. Then, she heard one of them yell about a horse that they saw in the distance. Victoria knew they had spotted Golden Sand, and soon enough they would spot her, too.

She frantically looked around for a better weapon or another escape route. The men were between her and the brook. To her back was a rock outcropping. Besides, they were already mounted and she would never get on Golden Sand and outrun them at this distance. She plotted her defense as they approached. Golden Sand whinnied and got to his feet as the men approached. Victoria whispered to him to calm him down.

Victoria could hear one of the men only a few horse paces from where she was hiding. He drew his sword, pointed it towards Golden Sand, and his horse trotted at a fast pace towards Victoria's location. He yelled in Victoria's direction, asking whether she was friend or foe, but Victoria knew they weren't friends. Instead of responding, she waited until the latest moment to make her move. Her grip on the stick she had used to poke at the fire tightened as she jumped away from the blackberry bushes, and waved it at the rebel man's horse. His horse jumped back in fear at the site of the hot, fiery stick and the desperate woman wielding it. It neighed and wildly kicked its front legs in the air, throwing the rebel man off his back. The man's sword flew from his hands, and landed near the bushes. Victoria grabbed the sword. The soldier had fallen on his chest, the wind knocked out of him. His hands fruitlessly groped the ground for his sword. He moaned in pain, unable to move more than his hands. His horse galloped about wildly, landing a heavy hoof right on the man's head. The man's hands collapsed at his side, suddenly still. The horse ran off, alerting the other men that something was amuck.

Victoria slowly approached the man, the sword held straight in front of her in fear that he might still somehow be alive. His face was now covered in mud and bright red blood. There was no doubt that he was indeed dead. She knelt down and held her hand to his face, closing his eyelids so he could die with some respect, but still thankful that this man could do her and Golden Sand no more harm.

At this point, the other mounted men were on their way towards Victoria. Adrenaline still pumping, she grabbed the sword sheath from the man that lay dead in front of her and took his sword with her for protection. Golden Sand was neighing loudly now. Victoria hopped on his back, tugged his reins and began racing off to avoid confrontation with the other men. They were not likely to have mercy on her given the fate of their friend. Her newly acquired sword dangled from her left side, rhythmically tapping her leg as Golden Sand galloped as fast as his legs would allow him.

Now it was a matter of outrunning the men. Victoria may have taken one of them by surprise but she knew she did not have the brute force or skill to take on the others. Her head, still slightly sore from her 'welcome' to the rebel camp, began throbbing. Victoria had to ignore this pain, for if she allowed Golden Sand to slow down, the rebel men would surely catch up and kill them.

Golden Sand pumped his legs as he galloped along the trail, the rebel men and their horses not too far behind. Up ahead, a steep ravine cut across the path. Victoria knew she had no choice but to try and jump the ravine to safety. If any of the three horses would be able to, Golden Sand would be the best bet. She held on tightly to the reins, anticipating a rough landing. Victoria shut her eyes as they jumped, and kept them tightly closed.

For a brief moment, Victoria felt as light as air. She opened her eyes, only to wish she hadn't. They were directly over the ravine, where a wild river flowed uncontrollably. It appeared for a terrifying moment that they would fall short, but then Golden Sand landed on the other side of the ravine. While she had felt weightless during the jump, the landing jarred her with an incredible force. It felt as if an explosion went off in her head, and Victoria wanted to scream. She bit her lip, literally biting back the pain until she could make sure they were safe. The other men and their horses had come to an abrupt halt at the ravine's edge. They had known they would be unable to make the jump, and they cussed and threatened her in their anger. Victoria turned towards the men, breathed deeply with relief, then turned Golden Sand and continued off down the trail towards Vhaldai.

Chapter XVIII

Michael had stolen a horse from the stable in the rebel camp. That had been nearly two weeks ago. The snow that once covered the entire land could only be found in small patches now. Birds began to sing their melodious songs, letting everyone know that they were here to stay until the next winter. Michael, having reached his destination, dismounted and slowly walked to the fortress that stretched out before him.

The high Moorg Mountains had some of the roughest terrain, but an experienced traveler could wind through the twists and turns of the mountainsides. Michael was such a traveler. Now, his gaze rested upon one of the safest Hemlock fortresses, protected by the surrounding mountains. This was GlenMoorg, where rumor said the Princess Victoria had retreated since the attack on Castle Hemlock. Michael now knew that the princess behind these walls was an imposter. Maybe the rumor had been started by the Hemlocks to fool the citizens while they searched for the princess themselves. Either way, if Michael was to find help for the princess on her travels, this would be the best place to find someone who just might believe his story.

"Halt and tell us the reason for your presence at GlenMoorg, traveler," shouted a guard to Michael as he approached the fortress.

Michael stopped and looked up to the tower where the guard was located. "I need to speak with someone," he started. "The princess is in trouble."

The guard seemed confused at this remark, then, "what sort of trouble do you suspect our princess to be in? Do you not believe her to be safe within our fortress walls?"

"She's not at this fortress," Michael confidently contradicted the guard. "She's traveling on her way to the city of Vhaldai."

With that, the guard's expression changed subtly. "Do not play games with me, young traveler. Our princess is safe within these walls. Do not speak such nonsense!" Michael sensed the shift in the guard's tone. He was on the defensive. Michael's claim had struck a nerve.

"You have to believe me!" he shouted back. "She is in great danger, even if she were to successfully make it to Vhaldai."

With that, a tower door to the fortress opened, revealing two guards. The guard in the tower informed the traveler that they did not have time for his crazy antics. The two gate guards came up to Michael, each grabbing an arm, and walked him towards the tower from which they came. Michael continued yelling towards the guard in the tower.

"Victoria is in danger! She needs our help! You can't just ignore me!"

He tried to break free of the guards and find someone who would listen to him, but they were stronger than he. He forced himself to stop struggling for the moment. He would need his energy to figure a way out of this situation. The guards led him down two flights of stairs in the tower. They opened an iron gate and pushed him inside. Michael stumbled inside and found himself within a damp cell strewn with a filthy, thin layer of straw that barely covered the stone floor. The gate was shut and locked before he could stand up and brush himself off. For the moment, Michael's journey had come to an abrupt end.

Chapter XIX

Victoria was lost. The two previous days had brought a tremendous spring downpour. While the land greedily soaked up what water it could, the excess had destroyed any remains of the trail that Victoria needed to find her way to Vhaldai. She was relieved that the rain was over, but it had left a mess for her to navigate. She had never been to Vhaldai before, and every bit of terrain that she and Golden Sand traveled appeared the same as the land they had passed only a few minutes before.

Exhausted and frustrated, Victoria sat down on a dry rock near a cluster of trees to think for a moment. Suddenly, out of nowhere, someone jumped out from the trees and landed on Golden Sand's saddle. This, of course, caused Golden Sand to jump and kick like a crazy horse. Victoria abruptly stood up and began yelling at the person to leave her horse alone, only to get knocked down when the unknown thief rode Golden Sand into the trees.

Victoria lost sight of Golden Sand, but could still hear him deeper in the woods. Despite not knowing what lie ahead, she dashed into the wild growth, pushing away loose limbs and branches that stuck in her way. Victoria was not about to lose the only traveling companion she had left. Without that horse, she'd never reach Vhaldi.

It took Victoria a minute or so of frantic back-and-forth searching, but she managed to come to a clearing on the other side of the trees where she had caught sight of Golden Sand. An unfamiliar young woman was sprawled on the ground next to Golden Sand. As Victoria watched warily, she stood up and brushed the dirt off her outfit. Golden Sand must have managed to knock her from his saddle, Victoria guessed. The thief wore a light brown tunic over dark brown pants. A shoddy crossbow was slung over her shoulder, and a red hat covered her head, making it impossible to tell her hair color.

Focusing intently on retrieving Golden Sand, Victoria stepped out into the clearing, only to be surprised to come face-to-face with a wild, raging river.

"Bring me back my horse!" shouted Victoria, unhappy with the events of the day, and anxious to get back on her way to Vhaldi.

The female, who seemed very bubbly despite being caught, giggled at her. "If you want him so bad, come and get him yourself!" She pointed up stream, where a makeshift dam attempted to tame the uncontrollable river.

Victoria, too angry to think before acting, walked down to the dam and looked it over. It was made of thick logs, placed together with little to no organization or attempt to permanently keep the river dammed. She grabbed the edge of her dress so as not to trip on it, and then slowly placed her left foot on one of the most secure looking logs.

Once she gained some balance, she lifted her right foot and placed it in front of her, performing her balancing act once again. The thief chuckled again. She seemed confident that Victoria would not reach her.

"You should have seen your horse clear that thing! What a silly thing to do!"

Victoria, irritated, told her, "if you like games so much, why don't you go for a fun little swim? Don't worry, I won't stop you."

The girl laughed, and then clapped her hands by her knees as if she were enjoying Victoria's predicament.

The thief then attempted to pull herself back onto Golden Sand's saddle, but he would have nothing more to do with her. He snorted loudly, tossed his head about wildly and stepped away from the stranger, throwing her off balance with each attempt to get back on the saddle. Victoria was too focused on keeping her balance to notice much of what was going on between them.

Victoria had finally made it to the other side of the dam, but when she looked up, the thief was gone. Victoria rolled her eyes, walked over to Golden Sand, and then patted him on the star on his head. Golden Sand's persistence must have driven her off. He gave a happy neigh, sensing that he was safe from the stranger's crazy games.

"Well, that was interesting," Victoria whispered to herself as she looked around to make certain that the thief had run off for good.

She looked up and down the river's edge, hoping to find some other way besides the crummy dam to cross to the other side. Unfortunately, the dam appeared to be their only option. She grabbed Golden Sand's reins and coaxed him to the edge of the dam, where she began edging across the slippery logs once again. Golden Sand followed reluctantly.

About halfway across, Victoria noticed something coming their way fast from up stream. She looked hard at the object, realizing it was a log caught in the fast moving current. That was when it became clear to Victoria that what she was standing on, in fact, was not a dam at all. Someone had been cutting down trees and using the river as a fast means to transport them, and these logs had simply managed to get stuck together to make what appeared to be a dam.

Victoria knew that she and Golden Sand were not safe; especially with another log plowing its way down the river. She began jumping across the logs as fast and as safely as she could, tugging Golden Sand along... Suddenly, her dress got caught on a short branch, causing her to lose her balance and nearly fall off the log structure.

As Victoria fell, she wrapped her arms around one of the large logs. She struggled back up, careful to maintain balance. She tried to free her dress from the branch, but somehow it had twisted just enough when she had fallen that it jammed the material between two large logs. She looked at the rapidly approaching log and realized that she wouldn't have time to make it to land before it made impact.

Immediately, Victoria released Golden Sand's reins and yelled at him to continue across. He tried, but kept losing his footing on the slick logs while trying to pass Victoria. He froze in a panic.

"Go! Go!" yelled Victoria, signaling to Golden Sand to hurry across.

It was too late. The log made impact, causing the rest of the structure to come apart. One by one, the logs were freed. Victoria was sucked into the cold, raging river along with her stallion. She tried to kick her legs and paddle her arms to keep on top of the river, but the logs around her made it nearly impossible. She heard Golden Sand neighing somewhere in the river by her, and she turned her head to look for him. Instead, she turned her head just in time to see a massive log coming in her direction. She had no time to react. The log struck her head and all went black.

Chapter XX

Victoria awoke to Golden Sand's cold nose nudging at her face in attempts to wake her up. She slowly opened her eyes, raising a weak hand to the stallion to give him a pat on the head. Her head felt like it had been split by an axe and she felt sick from the attempt to lift her head. She gave up for the moment, letting her hand drop back to the damp sand. Golden Sand walked away to munch on a patch of nearby grass.

Victoria lay there, tilting her head only a tiny fraction in order to catch a glimpse of her surroundings. The two had drifted to a calm area of the river, lucky enough to float to a small sandy area at the river's edge. The rest of the river bank was adorned with grass and wild spring flowers. Just beyond this, trees stood along the edge of the river, making it difficult to determine where exactly she was, not that she'd know anyway. Satisfied that she was at least alive and out of the river, Victoria closed her eyes and lost consciousness once again.

When she next awoke, she heard the sound of hooves slowly coming towards her. She lay there in a peaceful daze, figuring it was only Golden Sand roaming around for a wider variety of grasses to munch on. Then she heard a male voice speak.

"You don't see this very often," the voice said.

Victoria felt a chill down her spine. She tried to sit up as her eyes flew open, fearing that she may have been caught by rebels.

Then, "Wait, Victoria?"

Victoria turned her head towards the male speaker, now recognizing the voice as that of her youngest living brother,

Jean Kent Hemlock. She smiled weakly at him as she managed to struggle into a sitting position, her head still throbbing with pain, but better than before. Jean's golden brown hair and light brown eyes were a sight for sore eyes. He was at her side immediately, "Where are you hurt? What happened? How did you get to be here? Everyone's looking for you!"

Victoria held up a hand to still his questions. "Wait!" she affectionately admonished him. "One thing at a time. Let me look at you!" Victoria was amazed at the changes that had taken place since she last saw him a year ago. He was still a squire then, although close to Knighthood. Now, he wore an outfit of a similar mossy green color as Victoria's dress. Over this he also wore steel armor emblazoned with the royal coat of arms.

"My goodness, Victoria. You've changed so much since the last time I saw you. Your hair! It's so short!" Jean spoke, still in shock at having found his sister like this. Seeing her injured face, he gently wrapped his arms around her in an affectionate embrace. Victoria felt grateful and relieved. It had been a long time since she had seen any of her family, much too long.

Two palace soldiers emerged from the trees on horseback towards the reunited siblings. They were even more surprised than Jean to find Princess Victoria by the rivers' edge. They informed Jean that the other soldiers were making camp just a few hundred yards further into the forest. Jean thanked them, and asked Victoria to accompany him back to the camp. Victoria, weary from having traveled alone for so long, and from her injuries, was more than happy to accept.

Jean, who still could not believe that Victoria had traveled so far from Castle Hemlock on her own, peppered her with questions about her adventures. Victoria was more than happy to tell the tale. She began with the planned attack on Castle Hemlock, her daring escape, the new friend she had made on the trail, her experience in a rebel camp, and of their uncle's lies and deceit. Jean listened intently to every word.

Chapter XXI

Michael had been stuck in the jail cell for close to a week now. The damp environment had grown all too familiar to him, from the wet stone floors to the filthy straw covering it. Michael had made a bed by stacking the straw and had a single shoddy horse blanket for meager comfort. He had been given a single wooden drinking cup, which was filled with weak ale twice a day. On his own, Michael had devised a way to get more to drink by placing the cup in the back corner of his cell, beneath a drip in the stone ceiling. It served two functions: slaking his thirst and keeping the cell a bit drier than normal.

Michael sat on his makeshift straw bed, elbows on his knees; face cupped in his hands. The jail itself had grown quiet, and all Michael could hear was the dripping of the water as it fell into his cup. Then he heard the large wooden door that led out of the jail slowly swing open. The other prisoners in their cells began yelling at the visitor, engulfing the noise of the drippy ceiling. Michael was curious about the visitor, but didn't join in the ruckus.

"Hey, you, boy!" yelled a prison guard, banging on the bars of Michael's cell.

Michael looked up to see the prison guard. He had an old deer bone in his hand, which he had used to bang the bars of the cell. Once he had Michael's attention, the prison guard moved away, revealing two palace guards. A female figure nudged her way between the two guards. She smiled at him as she approached his cell.

"Victoria!" Michael gasped, abruptly standing up and grabbing the bars between them. A closer look at this figure before him, and Michael realized his mistake. She looked like

Victoria at first glance, but this woman had long hair and no sparkle in her eyes. "No, you're not Victoria," he said, letting go of the bars and taking a step back. "Who are you?" he asked.

"I'm Penny, Victoria's chambermaid," she replied. "It seems you already know that Victoria is not here. Once the guards informed me of your visit, I explained my story to them. With Victoria gone, it was decided by the castle staff that I would be her decoy in hopes of throwing off our enemy. With the help of the King's advisor, I have been given more decision making power until Victoria or another relative of the royal family returns."

"Victoria is in trouble!" Michael interrupted. He refused to be ignored this time. "She's heading to Vhaldai to find Prince Alejandro, but Vincent has plans to attack the city and take the throne for himself! She's in danger and needs our help!"

Penny listened intently to Michael's story. She knew Victoria had planned on finding the Prince, but she had no idea that Victoria would head toward war-torn Vhaldai. Penny was also curious to know who this Vincent was, or if it was the Vincent who was brother to the king. She could not ignore any possibilities of Victoria being in trouble. Knowing she had no other choice, Penny motioned to the prison guard to release Michael from his cell. The prison guard mumbled disapprovingly as he shuffled through a few sets of keys, but he then unlocked Michael's jail cell as directed. Michael stepped out of the cramped cell, happy to finally be free, but wary of what might happen next.

Penny had the two palace guards escort her and Michael to the royal sitting room, where the two sat down by a large fireplace to converse. Food and drink were brought to Michael as he began to tell his story, starting with when he first met Victoria. He told Penny of his last conversation with Victoria and how she had set off alone to find Vhaldai. Even though he had been a rebel when the movement started, he told everything he knew about them to Penny, including Vincent's treason to his family. He told of the great army Vincent had gathered, hundreds of times larger than the initial guesses made by the King's advisors.

Penny knew Vincent was a wise and cunning man, and if the stories Michael had told were true, then Victoria and her brothers were in great danger. Vhaldai, at this point in the war, had been cut off from all communication, so there was only one way left to save the remaining siblings of the Hemlock family. Penny stood up and turned towards the palace guards.

"Round up as many soldiers as possible," she told them firmly. "We're going to Vhaldai."

Chapter XXII

It had been nearly a week since Victoria and Jean had been reunited. Jean and his small army of one hundred Palace Soldiers were slowly making their way to Vhaldai in hopes of beating Vincent and his rebels to Alejandro. If no warning of the impending rebel attack reached Vhaldai before Vincent, then their chances of survival would be slim to none.

They were two days' travel from Vhaldai. Victoria awoke that morning to the sweet smell of spring air. The birds were calmly singing as Jean and his Palace Soldiers packed up their supplies to start off on the day's journey. Victoria couldn't help but hum along, as she reminisced about the similar melodies heard in the palace courtyard.

Victoria, though unable to do any heavy lifting, helped where she could. She made her way to a copse of trees where her horse and Jean's were secured to an old oak. Knowing of Victoria's uncanny way with horses, Jean had agreed to allow her to care for his own, an unusually shy stallion named Ash. He was black as coal, giving his brown eyes a mysterious appearance. At dusk, he became almost invisible in the shadows, and his eyes were often the only noticeable feature. Victoria had been around Ash before, back in the palace stables. Ash had recognized Victoria, and behaved better for her than he did for even Jean! Victoria had always been amazed at the way a horse's instincts could tell them if a person was friend or foe, stranger or familiar, despite appearances. If only she and her family possessed such instincts, they would have smelled out Vincent for the rat he truly was.

Once Ash was saddled up and ready for the journey, Victoria turned to Golden Sand. He had been waiting patiently for his turn. She carefully cupped his chin with her hand and gave him a kiss on his nose. Jean had offered her a "better" horse to ride, but she politely declined. After all, she and Golden Sand had shared so much together on this journey that she wouldn't dream of trading him in now. She finished saddling him up as Jean came by to inform her that it was time to head out.

Jean mounted Ash as a Palace Soldier yelled to him and pointed at a hill far off in the distance. Jean squinted in the distance while Victoria mounted Golden Sand. "Oh, God," was all Victoria heard Jean groan. "We're too late!"

In the distance, a rebel army numbering in the thousands was making its way across the land toward them They had obviously spotted the small camp of Palace Soldiers, as they were marching over the hill at a fast pace. Jean had to make a decision, and quick. Draw their swords and fight, or retreat until reinforcements could be summoned.

"Draw your swords and fight!" He yelled to his soldiers. "We may fight to the death, but we will fight for honor."

"What?" came Victoria's shocked reply. "If we fight, we will all die!"

"No," Jean told Victoria. "The soldiers and I will fight; you must go to Vhaldai and find Alejandro."

"You're outnumbered!"

"Will you do that for me?"

"It's a suicide mission!"

"Will you do that for me?" Jean shouted fiercely.

"No, I won't leave you to die! Not like the rest, not like Benson!" came Victoria's reply. She froze, as the memory of Benson's cold, dead body flashed through her head. "You'll all die," she whispered, almost to herself.

At this point, the Palace Soldiers had all drawn their swords and met up with the rebel army. A clash of metal rang out over the clearing where the Palace Soldiers' camp had once been. Everything to Victoria seemed so loud, so bright, so overwhelming to look at or even to think about. Then Jean reached out and put his arm on her left shoulder and everything seemed to stop, or to at least slow down. She refocused her attention on him and tried to understand what he was telling her.

"You have to do this for me, for us," he began. "Even if we reached Vhaldai, the city is not prepared to protect us from such an army. Not yet. If we had just one person who could reach Vhaldai and warn them, just one person who knew everything that the rebels were planning, then Vhaldai might be able to save themselves. You have been to a rebel camp. You have made a rebel friend and learned many secrets. Victoria, I need you. Alejandro needs you. Vhaldai needs you, but most important of all, your Kingdom needs you. Will you do this?"

Victoria's eyes swelled with tears. She couldn't reply because of the lump that had formed in her throat. Instead, she nodded in agreement, wiped a tear from her cheek, and rode off as fast as she could in the direction of Vhaldai. She did not once look back as Jean drew his sword and charged to battle. She held her head close to Golden Sand's mane as he galloped, tears streaming back from her eyes. She could not bring herself to look back, for she already knew Jean's fate. Yet another one of her brothers would die because of this terrible war. Her only consolation was knowing that Jean would die fighting in the hopes that she would live to save Vhaldai and the entire Hemlock Kingdom. Victoria couldn't let him down. No, she *wouldn't* let him down.

Chapter XXIII

Michael was amazed at the number of troops Penny had been able to gather, with the help of the King's advisor, in such a short amount of time. Nonetheless, they would still be grossly outnumbered by the rebel troops being sent to Vhaldai. Michael voiced his concern, but Penny reassured him that the palace warriors were highly trained and worth 5 rebels apiece.

Michael had been cooperating with Penny and the palace warriors to relay what information he knew regarding the rebels and their army. They were going over all possible scenarios of what could happen once they reached Vhaldai. Of course, this included the worst-case scenarios as well.

After deciding a few final details, everyone was dismissed to get some rest before heading out at dawn.

Michael exited the fortress, pushing aside the thick door that led to a balcony. He looked out at the familiar night sky. He had been a traveler a good portion of his life, but Victoria, a princess who had spent her life within the comfort and protection of the palace, was the one out there now. He was worried. Had Victoria survived the journey to Vhaldai, or had the elements or the rebels gotten to her first? Or was Victoria lost and all alone? There were endless possibilities, and Michael dreaded thinking about them. He shook his head as if to remove the terrible thoughts from his mind. Michael set off for some rest, as he knew he had to be in top form if there would be any hope of saving Vhaldai and Victoria.

Chapter XXIV

Victoria and Golden Sand had finally reached Vhaldai. Victoria felt a tremendous sense of relief closely followed by trepidation as she caught sight of her destination. Golden Sand had run nonstop for nearly a whole day while Victoria kept on high alert for any rebels on the trail. The pair was fortunate enough to not run into any of them, but it was an exhausting journey nonetheless. Victoria had very little energy left, and could only imagine how sore Golden Sand must be. Sheer will kept her going.

When the two arrived at the gate of the fortress in Vhaldai, Victoria dismounted Golden Sand. They approached the gate slowly, seemingly unnoticed. Eventually a guard spotted Victoria and called down to her, asking her purpose in Vhaldai. Victoria, as exhausted as she was, mumbled a response. Unable to understand her, the guard called down to her again. When a clear response did not follow, a guard was sent down to apprehend the intruder. Victoria found herself face-to-face with a formidable fortress guard.

The guard crossed his arms, and questioned Victoria in a commanding voice, "What is your purpose in Vhaldai?"

Victoria had difficulty forming her response. How to make them listen?

"Look," the guard told Victoria. "You can't enter the fortress without a good reason. I don't want to have to throw you back out there, but you must state your purpose here."

Victoria knew the guards would be skeptical if she told them who she really was right away. After all, a princess never travels alone, or at least that's what the guards would assume.

She had to come up with a decent story, one that would get her into Vhaldai until she could speak with brother, Alejandro.

"Prince Jean Hemlock sent me," she started. "I was to speak to Prince Alejandro about their current situation. There was a rebel attack and the Prince needed me to come here and inform his brother about the casualties."

"Prince Jean?" repeated the guard. He rubbed his chin for a moment while churning the story over in his head. "It sounds unlikely, but I cannot be the one to decide that." The guard took a look at Victoria and her horse, and then gave a wave in the direction of the gate. "Right this way missy. I'll see what I can do to get you an audience with Prince Alejandro. I can't make any promises, though. He's a busy man, as you might imagine!"

The gate opened, screeching loudly on rusted hinges as it was lifted up. The guard began walking into the fortress with Victoria and Golden Sand not far behind.

Chapter XXV

Victoria waited impatiently, pacing back and forth in the room she had been led to by the guard. The room had a couch with a dark putrid green color to it that was lightened by the strands of golden thread delicately woven into floral patterns throughout its cushions. There was another, larger couch with the same green color and golden weaves set diagonal to the first one. The floor, which was dark oak hardwood, was covered between the two couches with a deep red rug. Black and gold patterns adorned it. Two edges of the rug were decorated with tan tasseling. It was easy to see that this rug was old, its fabric worn down in several spots. Vhaldai, being a war-torn city, did not have luxury interior designing on the top of its to-do list.

Precious time was passing, and Victoria had only a vague idea of how much had already been wasted. She forced herself to sit on the couch in the royal sitting room of the Vhaldishian fortress and absentmindedly picked at some loose golden threads sticking out from the material.

Victoria's thoughts were brought back to the present by two male voices in an adjacent room. Though she could not distinguish their words, she immediately recognized her brother Alejandro's deep voice. She stood up from the little couch and proceeded towards the direction of the voices, stopping just short of the door leading into the adjoining chamber. From here, she could make out what they were saying. Victoria could tell that they were talking about her, about why Jean would have sent an unknown woman to Vhaldai instead of a palace guard. Though Alejandro wanted to speak with the unknown female to gain what information he could, the advisor concluded that it must be a trick, and that this unknown woman be sent away immediately. Victoria could not let that happen, so before the fortress guard could enter her room, she burst through the door to show Alejandro her true identity.

"Alejandro, please tell me you recognize me!" she said as the guard tried to block her from Alejandro.

Before the guard could take hold of Victoria to escort her out, Alejandro held his hand up to motion him to back away. He walked up to Victoria and stared her straight in the face. She did not look away. He had an almost menacing look to his face at first, but then it subsided. He backed off and, with barely any movement in his body, turned his attention to the guard.

"Have you any idea who this visitor might be?" Alejandro questioned him.

Victoria could feel her stomach quake. Was Alejandro unable to recognize her, his only sister? The fortress guard shook his head in simple response. Of course he did not know who she was. Why should he, when she spent most of her life surrounded by the palace guards and away from the distant fortresses? Victoria feared she might fail Jean after all. She took her gaze off of Alejandro and looked at her feet in shame.

"This, you numbskull, is my sister," Alejandro told the guard.

Victoria looked up in surprise. Alejandro had remembered her! He must have been pretending to be unsure. She smiled when she saw the mischievous grin on his handsome face and his arms opened in a welcome invitation. She ran to her brother to give him a big hug. The fortress guard bowed slightly and took up his post once again.

Alejandro gave his sister a hug back, and then looked intently at her from arm's length. His expression was one of humor, mixed with incredulity and concern.

"How in the world did you ever travel to Vhaldai on your own, little sister?" he asked Victoria.

"Well, I wasn't always on my own," she began.

Alejandro motioned for the guard to leave them alone. The two siblings made their way back to the sitting room so Victoria could tell Alejandro her story and the adventures she had endured, but most importantly so she could relay Jean's message. Alejandro hung on to every word, amazed that his little sister had succeeded in traveling this far from the safety of the palace walls. Victoria, though exhausted, was happy to be in the company of family once again.

Chapter XXVI

Victoria had spent the night in a guest room in the Vhaldishian fortress. The corridors in the fortress seemed almost never-ending. She had been placed just around the corner from Alejandro's quarters, which helped Victoria feel safer and more connected to her brother. She had been able to wash up, eat a good meal, catch up on some necessary sleep and slip into a new outfit made specifically for her by a tailor within the fortress. Her new outfit made her feel like herself again. It was the first time she had worn decent clothes since fleeing the castle. It was of a silky turquoise color that was even embroidered in lovely patterns with tiny turquoise stones from the top of the shoulders to just below her waist.

Alejandro had been busy since dawn. He had gathered all his commanders to discuss the details of the rebel army that Victoria had shared with him the previous day. He no longer wondered if war would break out at Vhaldai, but he still did not know when the attack would come. It became his responsibility to prepare his troops for battle, and hopefully for victory as well. Alejandro knew Victoria's words were not something to take lightly, especially since he had now learned that there was a traitor within the family.

Victoria had spent the majority of her morning in the little chapel just inside the fortress walls. She remembered the church within the palace walls and how she could find peace upon entering its doors. Even when her brothers' dead bodies lay within that church, she knew that they, too, had found peace. She hoped that Jean would do the same, whether he had survived his ordeal or his body lay on bloodied ground far from home.

Victoria gave the prayer that had become all too familiar to her in these times of war. She prayed for her people in the Hemlock Kingdom, for her brother to be safe and for the war to soon be over. She had almost left the church when she realized she had forgotten one person. She sat back at her bench and began another prayer.

"Please keep my friend, Michael, safe on his journeys. We may not be of the same class or hold the same beliefs, but he is still a good person who helped to keep me safe and protected me when I first journeyed outside the palace walls."

With that, Victoria headed off to find Alejandro to see where she could help in preparing for the battle that was soon to ensue.

Chapter XXVII

Penny, Michael and the GlenMoorg soldiers were making good time. They were not far from Vhaldai now. Michael could not help worrying about Victoria and the unknown. Nonetheless, he did his best to help Penny and the warriors despite his fears.

Penny and Michael had been traveling on horseback at the front of the GlenMoorg army. Michael navigated so as to avoid any unnecessary confrontation with the rebels. So far, the journey had been uneventful.

Then, the group came to a clearing. One of the soldiers had discovered a body lying in the road. Penny, Michael, and a few of the men dismounted to investigate the situation.

"It's a palace soldier," Penny remarked.

"I've found another over here!" came another voice. "This one appears to be a rebel."

They searched around the clearing to get a better idea of the situation. There were at least one hundred dead palace soldiers in the clearing along with a slightly greater amount of dead rebels. The ground was soaked with blood and dead horses lay among their fallen masters.

"The rebel army has already been through here," Penny stated. . "I haven't any idea where these palace soldiers came from, nor where the rest have gone to."

Penny and the soldiers considered the dead bodies as they discussed possible scenarios of what had happened. Michael began moving further into the battle zone. He hadn't realized the rebel army would be moving out this early. If he, a once loyal rebel, hadn't known this, then how would anyone at Vhaldai or the palace have known to send men to fight them off early? Something about this whole situation just didn't make sense.

Then Michael came across something out-of-place. The man looked like another soldier, except for the highly polished steel armor. Not even a palace soldier would have such fine armor. He approached the body for further inspection. Michael suddenly realized where these soldiers had come from.

"Prince Jean Hemlock is dead," Michael slowly whispered to himself. He bowed his head to pay his respects to the Prince of Hemlock.

Penny noticed Michael's unusual actions, and motioned her group to head to his position. When she reached Michael's side, she, too, knew who she was looking at. The news of Prince Jean's death began to spread quickly through the ranks. As it did, everyone bowed their heads or knelt in respect of their fallen Prince.

Penny and Michael both knew Jean deserved a proper burial, so a small group of soldiers was ordered to stay behind long enough to see that this happened. Penny spoke to the rest of the soldiers to rally them into moving on. Soon enough, they were back on their horses and ready to leave.

Before Michael left Jean's body to the loneliness of the blood-soaked battleground, he knelt by his side, removed his helmet, and closed his eyes. He stood up, looked around, and grasped Jean's sword that lay a few feet away. He placed the sword in Jean's hands and folded them across his chest. Jean was a true hero, and deserved to be treated as such.

There was no more time to waste, so Michael mounted his horse and nodded towards Penny, who had been waiting. Penny, Michael and the GlenMoorg army headed off in the direction of Vhaldai, hoping to get there before the rebels could do any further harm to the remaining children of the Hemlock Kingdom.

Chapter XXVIII

The sun was now starting to sink below the horizon. There was a light breeze that did nothing to disturb the tense atmosphere that had settled over Vhaldai. Victoria stood at the top of the fortress walls, looking down at the mass of soldiers Alejandro had managed to conjure up. They were inside the walls of the Vhaldishian fortress, waiting for the rebel army that was quickly approaching. Though the sky was completely clear, a thunderous sound could be heard rolling in from the distance. The rebel army was near.

Victoria looked down to where her brother Alejandro stood. He was behind his soldiers, ready to give commands at a moment's notice. He was on horseback, adorned in a metal armor similar to that which his soldiers wore. Victoria gave a half-smile. It was just like Alejandro to associate so well with his soldiers that he would even dress like them.

She looked in the distance at the setting sun. Victoria knew the growing shadow near the horizon was not just caused by the setting sun, but rather the rebel army approaching in the distance. They were finally here. She looked over her right shoulder at the soldiers who were positioned with arrows on the wall alongside her. Victoria could tell they were anxious. Not a single one made a sound.

Suddenly, she heard a booming roar coming from the soldiers below the wall. She looked down at her brother again, who had his hand on his sword. Alejandro was rallying his soldiers for battle. Victoria had faith in her brother, and she could tell that his men did as well.

The rebel army was closing in. The soldiers nearest Victoria drew an arrow from their quivers and readied their bows for fire. Alejandro and the soldiers stood at the ready should the rebels break through the fortress wall. The soldiers on the wall began firing their arrows as the rebels began making their attempts to overrun the fortress.

Victoria watched in dread as wave after wave of rebel men made their attempt to break the wall. Trebuchets easily flung massive boulders high in the air while a ram was used in an attempt to knock the gate down. With so many rebels outnumbering the soldiers on the wall, it didn't take long for the gates to come down.

Alejandro drew his sword and the fortress soldiers followed. He raised his sword high in the air, and then pointed it towards the enemy. If the rebels wanted this fortress that bad, they would have to fight tooth and nail for it. The soldiers on the ground drew their swords and rushed forward, meeting with the swarm of rebels that had already penetrated the fortress. A clash of metal on metal rang out.

It was painful to watch. Victoria covered her ears in a vain effort to keep out the cacophony of noise from the battle. Mixed in with the meeting of swords were screams of fury and shouts of pain. Men from both sides fell to their doom. Victoria did her best to keep her eye on her brother.

Alejandro was an amazing fighter. Victoria watched as he deftly guided his horse between the brawling men on the battlefield. He stopped his horse, turned slightly to his right, and plunged his sword into the chest of a rebel. Next, he swung his sword around to his left and slashed the throat of yet another. He ran his horse further into the sea of battle and continued slashing, gashing and lacerating the enemy.

Victoria heard one of the soldiers standing to her left yell out. She was so focused on keeping an eye on Alejandro that she hadn't heard what he had said. Suddenly, a hail of arrows came pouring down on them from the enemies on the ground. One of the soldiers grabbed Victoria and pulled her behind the wall, away from the raining arrows. He raised his shield to protect her from the deadly volley. Once the barrage ceased, Victoria abruptly stood up and looked out over the wall.

She had lost sight of her brother, who blended in with the other men fighting on the ground. Victoria's eyes darted back and forth, trying to catch sight of him.

"Incoming!" Victoria heard the warning just as another barrage of arrows was launched by the enemy. Victoria knew she was no longer safe on the fortress wall, so she ducked under cover to wait for the arrows to fall. When it was safe, she quickly darted away.

Inside the fortress, Victoria could still hear the sounds of the battle. Unfamiliar with the fortress, she began searching for a safe place, without knowing exactly where to go. There were a few soldiers running through the hallways, yelling orders to others or heading off to relay messages to areas cut off by the fighting. Victoria could tell by the shouting that the rebels were winning.

Victoria heard a familiar voice in the hallway. She turned around to see Alejandro with two soldiers marching beside him. He gave them both an order, and they darted off in separate directions. Alejandro, who had retreated into the fortress in order to better direct the battle, almost walked right past Victoria.

Alejandro seemed worried. He gripped Victoria by both shoulders and looked straight into her eyes.

"I need you to head back to your quarters," he told Victoria. "The rebels are breaking through our defenses. I don't want you caught in the crossfire."

Victoria felt a sense of defeat. Had she come this far, through so many trials, just to see her brother defeated, completing the loss of the Kingdom? A knot formed in her throat, preventing her from speaking. Instead, she nodded her head in agreement. Tears began to swell up in her eyes.

"Good," Alejandro replied as he gave a nod back in approval. He dropped his hands from Victoria's shoulders, turned around and continued on his way.

Victoria watched as Alejandro disappeared deeper into the fortress. She feared that his fate would end up just the same as Jean's. Victoria did not want to leave yet another one of her brothers behind to fight for her survival, but she knew she was not a fighter. Mustering her resolve, she made her way to her rooms.

Chapter XXIX

Victoria had been in her room for only a few minutes, but it had seemed like an eternity. There had been no sign of anyone, but she could hear footsteps and yells of the occasional fortress soldier outside her quarters. She sat in the corner of the room with her head resting on her knees.

Suddenly, the shouts of numerous soldiers came from outside her room. She strained to hear their words. The rebels had overwhelmed the defenses of the Vhaldishian fortress. Victoria instantly stood up, unsure of what to do.

A sword fight had erupted in the hallway. She knew she could not leave now. It was too late for that. She looked around her room, and her eyes fell upon a cherry wood chest across from her. She ran to it, opened it up, and pulled out the old sword she had acquired earlier on her journey. She had stored it there upon arriving at these new living quarters, but knew she may need the sword now. She pulled the sword from its sheath and looked in the direction of the door. Victoria was expecting the rebels to come through the door any minute now.

The door burst open, revealing the back of a male figure. Victoria raised her sword, preparing to attack the intruder.

The figure turned around, revealing that it was Alejandro. Victoria stopped herself mid-swing, shocked to find that Alejandro was still safe.

"Alejandro!" she cried warmly. "What's happening? I thought the rebels were here!"

Alejandro didn't have time to comfort her or answer her questions. He looked gravely serious, and for the first time, a bit fearful. He grabbed Victoria's arm and led her over the bodies of two rebels outside the door and down the hallway.

Victoria, still nervously clenching the sword in one hand, noticed someone following her and her brother, but her brother seemed unconcerned, so she didn't pay him much attention.

Chapter XXX

The situation at Vhaldai seemed impossible. Not only had the rebels penetrated the walls of the fortress, but they far outnumbered the fortress soldiers as well. The Vhaldishian army began to lose all hope.

Then, something miraculous happened. Far off in the distance, a river of warriors began to make its way toward Vhaldai. At first, it was assumed that this was yet another wave of rebels, but soon enough it was evident to the fortress soldiers that it was a Hemlock army. They had marched all the way from the high Moorg Mountains under the leadership of Penny, a servant from the palace who had been given the amazing opportunity to act as princess. Standing by her side was Michael, a former rebel who befriended the true princess of the Hemlock Kingdom and was changed forever by her kindness.

They rushed the field of battle and turned the tide of the war. Suddenly, the rebel numbers, though still superior, seemed unimportant. The Hemlock soldiers came as fast and as furious as a flood, engaging the already weary rebels like a crash of waves against a rocky shore.

Penny, Michael and a few GlenMoorg soldiers were intent on finding Alejandro and securing his safety. While they searched for the Prince, Michael saw ample evidence that Victoria had successfully made it to Vhaldai to warn Alejandro about the rebels. Michael felt relief and gratitude when he realized that Victoria had made it safely, but he had no way of knowing whether she was still safe. The small group began fighting their way into the fortress walls to begin their arduous search.

Chapter XXXI

With no safe place to run to, Alejandro and Victoria found themselves cornered in a large, open room. There were decorations covering the walls of the room along with a few chairs dispersed about. Alejandro ran to the end of room, but there was no exit. Victoria stood in the center of the room, watching the door they had entered as Alejandro frantically looked around.

Three men walked into the room, the sound of their footsteps unnerving to Victoria. Victoria recognized one of them as her uncle, Vincent. Alejandro had already drawn his sword. He walked in front of Victoria and pointed it towards his uncle.

"You're a traitor to your kingdom!" Alejandro accused Vincent, contempt in his voice.

Vincent simply smiled, and then his expression became serious. "You're the only thing in my way to that throne. You, and your little sister there," he said, his gaze falling first on Victoria, then back on Alejandro.

Vincent and his personal guards drew their swords. The two men lunged at Alejandro. Victoria backed away as she watched Alejandro dodge the attacks. He swung his sword around, ducked below the blade of one rebel, and plunged his own straight into the man's chest. Alejandro pushed his foot against the now lifeless body to extract his sword. He did this just in time to block an incoming blow from the second rebel. Alejandro used his forearm to shove the man backwards. As the rebel attempted to regain balance, Alejandro spun around and swung his sword, landing it deep into the man's side. Both of the rebel men had fallen to the ground, defeated.

Vincent was upset by his men's easy defeat, and he swung at Alejandro's exposed back in anger... Victoria screamed just in time for Alejandro to turn around and block the blow, but it had caught him off-guard and his sword clattered to the ground. Vincent was happy to take this opportunity to defeat his nephew. He raised his sword high above his head, preparing for the killing blow.

"The throne will be mine!" he yelled in a deranged, victorious voice. Vincent swung a deadly blow directly at Alejandro.

"No!" shouted Victoria as she instinctively took an offensive stance and swung her sword between Alejandro and Vincent. She managed to block Vincent's attack. She felt a throbbing pain pulse through her arms as the two swords clashed. She was not a fighter, and Vincent knew it.

Vincent turned to Victoria in a rage. He released his right hand from his sword, made a fist, and pummeled Victoria in the face. She fell backwards, her sword landing next to Alejandro.

Alejandro was able to grab Victoria's sword, roll away from Vincent and rise to his feet. He did this just as Vincent turned around to strike again. Alejandro raised his sword to block him.

Victoria was in a fog of pain. Her head felt split from the beating her uncle had given her face. She sat on her knees, one hand holding the ground to keep her balance and one hand gingerly exploring her temple. She felt a warm liquid and put her fingers in front of her eyes to inspect them. She felt faint as she saw bright red blood. She could hear the clash of swords as her brother and uncle continued to battle.

Victoria did her best to rise to her feet. She half-turned and saw that Alejandro had once again been unarmed. He was pinned against a wall, Vincent's sword at his throat. He said something to Alejandro that Victoria could not hear, and drew his sword to his side to deliver a final blow.

Victoria could not bear to let this happen. She had traveled too far, witnessed too much death and lost too many brothers to lose now. With every bit of strength and courage, she ran at Vincent with full force. Vincent did not notice Victoria until it was too late. She successfully knocked him off balance. As the two fell to the ground, Vincent's sword flew from his hands and clattered across the floor.

Alejandro recovered his sword while Vincent was down. Vincent attempted to stand up, but he fell over Victoria as Alejandro advanced. Victoria remained on the floor, dazed for the moment. She watched as Alejandro placed a foot on Vincent's chest and pointed his sword at his throat.

"It's over, Vincent," Alejandro told him.

Victoria, still lying on the ground, let out a shaky sigh of relief. She lifted her hand from her stomach to brush her hair from her eyes, and froze as she realized something was very wrong. Her hand was covered in blood. She stared at it, confused. It was not the same hand that had touched her injured face. So where had the blood come from? Then a sharp pain shot from her stomach, and she knew Vincent's sword had sliced her when she charged him.

At that moment, another group of people entered the room. Alejandro spoke to them as if they were friend rather than foe. She couldn't understand what he was saying through her daze as she lay there, bleeding. She was paralyzed with fear and pain. She did not know the extent of her injuries.

Two of the people rushed over to her. One of them lifted her hand from the ground. She turned her head and recognized Penny. She smiled weakly and looked at the other person. She couldn't believe her eyes.

"Michael, is that really you?" she forced herself to say, although it hurt so much to talk.

Michael smiled at her and nodded his head. "You didn't really think I was going to let you fight these rebels by yourself, did you?"

Victoria started to laugh, but it was extremely painful. She cried out, and Michael used his free hand to rest on the side of Victoria's face. She looked up at him and tried to stay focused on his kind eyes and warm hand as she battled to remain conscious.

"We have help coming, Victoria," Michael told her. "Just hold on for a bit longer." Victoria could tell that he was holding back tears.

There was chaos in the large, open room. Everything was going dark. She could still hear Michael talking to her, but she could no longer understand his words. She heard footsteps all around her, and she saw another shadow kneel by her side. Another sharp pain shot through her abdomen; then all went dark.

Chapter XXXII

The victory at Vhaldai led to exuberant celebrations. Weeks after the victory, the celebrations were still going strong. There was a constant supply of food, drinks and entertainment for all who came. Not an expense was spared and many from around the Hemlock Kingdom came to celebrate the defeat of the rebels and the peaceful and prosperous future that was sure to come.

Victoria dressed in a delightful lavender gown that flowed elegantly when she walked. Though she still was in pain from her battle wound, she was doing much better. Michael and Penny had been able to find the Vhaldishian doctor and have him safely escorted to the room where she lay. If Michael hadn't alerted Penny to the rebel attack, Victoria and Alejandro may well have died, giving Vincent control of the throne and limitless power.

She found Alejandro conversing with a few of the Vhaldishian soldiers. Since the victory, she hadn't had a chance to spend much time with her brother. She couldn't hear what the group was discussing, but she could tell that Alejandro was enjoying the celebrations. Victoria approached Alejandro, who dismissed himself from the conversation. The two walked away from the hustle and bustle of the celebrations to a quiet spot in the courtyard.

"You were quite impressive, Victoria," Alejandro began. "Journeying all the way to Vhaldai just to find your oldest brother." Alejandro gave a small smirk, and then his face became serious. "You have the qualities of a great ruler, Victoria."

"Perhaps," Victoria started, "But you were able to gather your soldiers and protect Vhaldai from the rebels until reinforcements could back us up. You, too, have the qualities of a great ruler and father saw this in you. That is why he chose you for the throne. He would have been so proud."

With these words, Alejandro smiled. "Glad to hear you won't be planning any rebellions against me."

Victoria giggled slightly, and then looked out the adjacent window at the winding Vhaldishian River. At this moment, Michael had walked into the courtyard, escaping the roar of the celebrations.

"Sir Michael James Rundy," Alejandro addressed him formally, but with a friendly twinkle in his eye. "Your Highness," came his reply. Michael bowed his head down in respect, showing the same level of formality mixed with friendliness as Alejandro.

Victoria smiled at this. After the battle was over and Vhaldai was saved, Michael had been given the opportunity of Knighthood in honor of all he had done for the Hemlock Kingdom. Although he had misgivings at first, Victoria had coaxed him into taking the title of nobility. It was an unparalleled honor and a chance to further serve in honor of his mother's memory.

"Would you mind if I took a moment of this lady's time?" Michael asked Alejandro. Alejandro did not mind, and took his leave to return to the celebration. Once he had left, Michael turned his attention to Victoria.

"I see you're doing better," he told her.

"Yes, thanks to you and Penny," came Victoria's reply.

The two stood there silently for a few moments. Victoria noticed Michael looking out the window at the Vhaldishian River, lost in thought. She knew he had spread his mother's ashes on the river just earlier that day and wondered if he was thinking of her now.

"Your mother would be proud of you," she told Michael, smiling warmly at him

Michael gave Victoria a half-smile.

"I mean it," she continued. "Not only did you fulfill her final request, but you even managed to save an entire kingdom in the process. I don't know a single person who wouldn't be proud of that."

"You saved the kingdom, too," Michael began. "You braved your first journey outside the palace walls to find your oldest brother and save Vhaldai from a rebel army that was plotting against it. I don't know a single person who wouldn't be proud of that. Your father would have been proud of you." He looked up at Victoria. "Prince Jean would have been proud of you."

Victoria's smile faded and she looked sad for a moment. . "You really think so?" she asked him.

"I know so," he responded.

Michael held his hand out and bowed his head to Victoria. "Would her highness join me in a dance?" he asked her.

Victoria held her abdomen, still sore from her injury. "I would love to," she began, "but I believe my body has suffered enough for a while. Perhaps a peaceful walk down to the river's edge instead?"

Michael smiled and took the hand that Victoria held out to him. They headed down the corridor together, happily chatting along the way.

Today was a marvelous day for the Hemlock Kingdom. The rebels had lost the most important battle of the war and would soon be run out of the Hemlock Kingdom altogether. A new and magnificent king was about to take the throne and bring peace back to the kingdom after years of terrible turmoil. To top it all off, the horrible Vincent Randall Hemlock had been exiled and had no further possibility of gaining the throne. Yes, it was a marvelous day for the Hemlock Kingdom indeed.

The End

Acknowledgements

I would like to thank my family for giving me the encouragement to write, my oldest brother, Kevin, for resurrecting my book from the hard drive of my previous laptop that crashed, and my parents, Dave and Roberta, and little brother, Kyle, for being my "book advisory committee."

Andrea Rose
Michigan
May 2011

About the Author

Andrea Rose has been writing stories since the moment she could pick up a writing utensil. She has always had an enchanting imagination and has continuously participated in groups and competitions stimulating her creative power, including Destination Imagination. She is currently a university student studying Forensic Science and will be a graduate December 2011. This is her first book, but she doesn't plan on stopping there. Andrea continues to pursue her passion for writing.

The Great Journey
A Legacy Continued

Release date: (Winter 2011/12)

Three years have passed. Peace has returned to the lands of Hemlock. Victoria continues her duties as Princess of Hemlock while Alejandro diligently serves as King. During one of Alejandro's peace visits to a neighboring realm, he becomes mysteriously ill. Victoria sets out to find a cure in the hopes of saving relationships at the highest levels of power. Will she be successful in her endeavors, or will war and strife return?